CW00501500

Atom's Walk

A novel by

Sarah Fretwell-Jex

First published January 2018.

Also by Sarah Fretwell-Jex

Xenophobia, published October 2017
The House on Every Corner, available in 2018

Acknowledgements:

I started writing this novel about a month before my dear father George Fretwell died suddenly and unexpectedly. It is a great comfort to me that he read the first six chapters hot off the press and gently pointed out that I had an apostrophe in the wrong place. Sorry you didn't read the rest! This book would never have happened without the encouragement and inspiration of Rory Patton, Cerys Evans, Bunty Clark, Kingsley Clark, Helen Tulley, Kathryn M Holford, Gill Orsman, Mark Bouch, Darren Eden and The Transformation, the beautiful Sussex countryside and NaNoWriMo.

Thank you all!

CONTENTS

(Beginning) In the beginning there were two Atoms that should have been drawn to each other by the very fact that there actually was nothing else.

Chapter 1: **The Path**

The air was fresh and clear and the sky seemed supra-luminescent, pouring determined beams of light down from an even more determined sun, into the darkest recesses of every part of the wood that ran along the side of the road. The relentless hum of speeding traffic did nothing to deter the joggers, walkers, cyclists and that little Old Boy on his mobility scooter, from making the best possible use of the new running track that would take them up to the very top of the road, to that poignantly sad place over the busy A27, only to be cut short, mid-stride, and forced by traffic to turn and return thwarted, back down the hill.

It was clear that every one of the track's participants had a script running in their head, that they were scrolling through in preparation for their day, processing and planning or justifying their next step out into the world, all in preparation for something, whatever was coming next. I can see those thoughts as I pass through.

That felt heavy; that felt light; that kind of buzzed as I passed through. The vibration of life was what really hit the spot and kept up the determined search for the next opportunity to engage with someone or something, which frankly was never more than a nanosecond away.

Coming up behind that redhead, with the amazingly fluid stride and diving into the fragrance of her hair, which always sent a scintillating pheromone out that drove the opposite sex wild, was something to be savoured. The Crow man was of interest too, the way he remained oblivious to anyone or anything other than the crows that he'd come out to feed and commune with, like old friends reincarnated. If someone called his name and said a friendly "hello", there'd be engagement momentarily and a smile, but nothing to take him away from his clear objective.

The lack of flesh on his poor old bones, under those ungainly but somewhat dapper charity shop clothes, was a stark contrast to the red-head who'd just passed him on the track in her shiny and thinly stretched Lycra. It's 7am. What a delightful view from up here, on such a sunny morning.

To the right, the Golf course, with it's rolling greens that seemingly touch the brilliant blue sky from this low point on the undulating path and to the left the gliterati of cars in the car park of the industrial estate. Cars like jewels in the sun, shining sufficiently to indicate their internal capacity for burning up energy, showing their potential for it as a far-off twinkle. No doubting your impact, my little metal friends.

Moving along The Path, it's too easy to be distracted and attention is drawn to the tiding of 12 Magpies cartoon bouncing about on the newly mown meadow grass to the left, just after the wood comes to an end and attention then quickly drawn to the right, as a gaggle of golfers wander over the perfectly manicured curve of grass, cutting out the sunlight one by one like an oscilloscope, with dizzying effect. Their movement rendered into slow-motion by the flashing of dark and light, dark and light, dark and light in starkest contrast, at least until the sun reaches sufficient sky-height for it to stop.

Here he is again, the beautiful boy from northern Portugal, who knows that there are better places than this to live his life, he's tasted love and seen the beauty that has to be seen, to bring himself truly to life and experienced hunger and despair that rendered everything all the more poignantly magnificent, because of the absolute contrast. Existential moments made all the more vivid by hormones and idealism. He runs here every day, wishing that he could keep on going, never looking back until he reaches paradise on earth. Passing through, his yearning is very real and the energetic motivation that is building in his every fibre is tangible and will take him very far away, very soon, but for now, for today, he is building tone and muscle for the journey that he's planning in his heart. He is strong and almost ready for the long journey ahead.

The Eco-terrorists and their Eco-dog 'E', who haunt the woods, believing themselves invisible. Maybe in their own heads, but I know what they're planning. Nothing anyone else does will ever be good enough for them. They think that they're here to save The Earth, but what they have overlooked is that The Earth doesn't need saving...it's the people and the plants, the bees and the beasts that need saving. The planet will just shrug them all off and get on with the business of dashing across the Universe in search of tomorrow. They seem to like disliking what others do in their endeavours to do their bit for this small community and take pleasure in their imagined invisibility, as they creep through the darker recesses of the wood, undoing the good work and laughing like ungrateful Goblins on their way home. Sometimes they walk The Path too, but only when they believe themselves alone, as they cannot bear to share. They wait 'til dusk or come out at dawn, hoping to keep up the myth that some unknown force is dismantling the bee hotels that were lovingly constructed at the bases of trees, chucking broken bricks about all over the carefully

7

cleared pathway that wriggles through the wood at the side of The Path.

Out again, Tall Girl, who gets taller every time she runs The Path, because she runs every day and has decided not to nourish herself sufficiently, so her bodily proportions are changing back to those that she cherished as a much younger tall girl. The fat years are behind her now and the steely determination that is tangible when I pass through, will never leave. Thin is in.

From the industrial estate, comes a line of three, men all and focused on the end result of being the best, better than the rest back at base and unstoppable as they jog, jog, jog, turn the corner once, jog, jog, jog and turn the corner twice in perfect formation, until they hit The Path and crunching in unison on the grit, they keep up a pace that others cannot match. One is struggling, that much is obvious as I pass through, but he hides it well. The others will never notice, so long as he can keep up the façade. He will keep it up because he is a real man, not a wimp. Passing through, picking up the tension in all three, something is about to break in their world, something that is coming their way whether they like it or not and they somehow know that it's coming because they've been assigned a difficult duty that will test their strength of character as much as their bodies.

They are a team, a team of three and they will stick together through thick and thin. They will win.

A distant spec is advancing, a lone jogger with uncertain gait, he's new to this game. Pale Physics Student, defying convention, escaping the lab, escaping the lecture theatre and jogging The Path, headphones in. This boy's going somewhere and though jogging is not his thing, his focus is clear, he wants to win the main prize. Diving in to get a whiff of the music that a physics student might listen to in order to relax and get away from his studies, unexpectedly it's not music, it's…French " à trois heures de l'après-midi", and to be an apprentice at Cern, Switzerland his ambition. Clever boy. He'll be jogging The Path a lot this year, his final year, as he learns both French and German with a hunger that will not let him down. The sun is starting to rise in the sky, leaving behind the oscillating long shadows on the grass, that fade to nothing as it rises further still in the sky, ready to mildly bake the users of The Path in the autumn sun, accompanied by the relentless dull, rattly, rhythm of the passing trucks and cars.

Chapter 2: **Damp Squib**

Same path, always the same path. Next day and the previous clarity that intense sunshine brings, is gone. There is drizzly and persistent rain. It is forming itself into waves, as if upon the shore they land, as the gusty winds blow in from the West. The few that have braved The Path this morning come huddled under hoods against the driving dampness, determined not to scupper their regime, keeping an eye on the prize: the perfect beach body for Sharm el Sheikh this Christmas, not a repeat of the flabby spread that had shamed her two years before; Remembering his fluffy companion whom he'd walked every day, come rain or shine and in whose honour he'd kept up the tradition; The promise that they'd made themselves last New Year, big sister's words still ringing in her ears that "you don't have what it takes to finish anything you've ever started, I'll give it three months", but she'd gone three months and more, she'd done 10 months and was into the eleventh and intended to go the whole 12, all the way to New Year's Eve. The energetic misery of these determined folk, like grit in an oyster, is tangible and growing. Nothing will stop them I determine, as I pass through. Others wish that they were on The Path this morning, but are less determined, less driven by some inner misery and rather better motivated by the joy that they feel stepping out under clear blue skies, fair-weather path-dwellers, driven by more optimistic thoughts, yet fragile in their own ways.

The wetness thins as the wind changes its energy from gusty to gentle and the raising of the temperature by just a degree or two brings a lightness to the wind, that separates out the larger drops into a gentle smur. Hope hangs in this gentle dampness and other users of The Path prepare to step out.

It is a busy day of preparation. It's difficult to miss the constant shuffle of people and endless bits of old wood of all shapes and sizes, being dragged hither and thither into two cairn-sized piles in the middle of the meadow. The piles increase throughout the day as locals gratefully bring out their dead for incineration. Broken furniture and garden choppings and clippings that have dried sufficiently to add fuel to the fires planned for later tonight. As I pass through I know that the man in the old Barbour jacket is smuggling in newly cut damp wood that he's been paid to chop and take away, in the hope that he can get rid of it for free. Getting it into the pile as early as possible in the day of gathering the wood, for it to be buried deep enough down so that nobody will notice its green pallor before the match is struck. He thinks the rules don't apply to him.

The smur thins and the day dries up, but a low fog lingers in pockets on the golf course and in the lowest edge of the meadow. Who's this on the edge of the wood? Lingering like the remaining mists, as the day's light begins to fade, camera in hand, seemingly looking for something where there is nothing of note. Looking through a lens, to both see and capture the unseen. Watch out Eco-warriors, she'll catch up with you and reveal your under-cover antics, you'll be captured forever in her discontinued Canon PowerShot A650 IS12 mega pixel digital...but actually they are not her intended subject, which I learn now as I pass on through to find out why she's here. This ritual has happened before, in fact every year that I have witnessed and many more that I have not. Fire is seemingly essential in these countries of the northern hemisphere, where the cold and damp of the autumn and winter gets deep into the joints and bones and lingers in them long into the spring. The pyres are built, like so many others across the country in every County; on village greens and in many private gardens as well. There will be trouble everywhere tonight, there is tension now, there will be a colossal wastage of fuel and an expenditure of much energy, as nature and man and the alchemical collide, going up in a blaze of glory, girded round by the illusory safety of woolly hats, gloves, hot dogs, baked potatoes and chilli. The very prospect of it all is thrilling,

12

resonating within me and raising my internal vibration to new and dizzying heights, but why I feel this excited is not yet clear. But it does have the ring of destiny about it.

As the first fire is lit something starts to happen, which I witness as I pass through. There is a buzz of excitement at all bonfire sites across the country, an air of anticipation. Wherever the gathering, the same thing is happening. People shuffling further forwards, or further back, depending on how safe or unsafe they feel and some irrational flurries of bravado run through the crowds. There is some pushing and a general jostling for position. Pale Physics student is here and as I pass through, I instantly know that Carbon dioxide emissions stem from the burning of fossil fuels. It's also produced during the consumption of solid, liquid, and gas fuels. There will be extra carbon emissions tonight. Maybe bonfire night is to blame for global warming? He muses.

This student has a head full of questions and amusing facts, so I pass through again to see what else I can pick up. You never can tell what you might find lurking in the darkest recesses of a mind, until you plunder its depths.
Fossil fuels, I learn, are formed by natural processes such as the anaerobic decomposition of buried dead organisms. The age of the organisms and their resulting fossil fuel is

typically millions of years and sometimes exceeds 650 million years. They contain high percentages of carbon and include coal, petroleum and natural gas. Other more commonly used derivatives of fossil fuels include kerosene and propane. There is kerosene here tonight, he's seen the can and already decided to move away from it, far, far away from it!

Although fossil fuels are continually being formed via natural processes, they are generally considered to be non-renewable resources because they take millions of years to form and the known viable reserves are being depleted much faster than new ones are being made. I know this already as I've been in the ether since the dawn of time. I have witnessed the ravaging of resources in a rather dispassionate and unconnected manner, but something about entering this young, energetic mind is bringing the visions all flooding back and I have a twinge of conscience and something else that I cannot quite put into place.

Back on through one more time I pick up on the last threads of his thinking in this vein tonight. The use of fossil fuels raises serious environmental concerns. Pale Physics student is momentarily concerned.

The burning of fossil fuels produces around 21.3 billion tonnes of carbon dioxide per year, but it is estimated that natural processes can only absorb about half of that amount.

It is one of the greenhouse gases that contributes to global warming, causing the average surface temperature of the Earth to rise in response, which the vast majority of climate scientists agree will cause major adverse effects. Major adverse effects. Well, that's nothing new. From what I have witnessed, that's par for the course with this lot, but somehow, passing through has filled me with an ambivalence combining both interest and anxiety, which is a new experience for me. I know that in reality I've picked up on the energy of Pale Physics students' own concerns. He's still young and although so very certain about some things, is also genuinely frightened that he doesn't really know so very much at all, given the increasing enormity of the bigger picture. I leave him to his anxiety.

Men are in charge tonight, they gather at the side of The Path, as if to protect the passing cars from what they are about to do, like the Gunpowder plotters but rather more visible, creating a human shield to deter the speeding passers-by from viewing the planned evenings entertainment. They cluster and in whispers, discuss the finer details of how best to get these fires started, as though their audience have no clue of what is to come.

I pass through and know that Man 1 is in charge of the matches, Man 2 the fuel, Man 3 and 4 are to herd the masses and keep them safe, while Man 5, 6, & 7 must block access from The Path, since all of 'The Invited' live below The Path at the side of the meadow and would therefore come in from below the meadow side. Their other concern is to do with another team of Men, who are in charge of the bombs. If this is the A-team, then they most definitely are the B for bomb team!

In the Police HQ and detention centre, on the edge of the Industrial estate, a line of three entirely Other Men sit waiting, on ready alert, a special SWAT team whose role it is to respond as quickly as possible to the expected emergencies of the evening. They all love and hate tonight in equal measure. I pass through and can feel the vibration created by the latent adrenalin already pumping through their blood. They have trained together and are ready for 'anything'. Past experience tells them that tempers run high on a night such as this. When men have little or no regular opportunity to set fire to things and let off bombs in their normal lives, they can easily get carried away and go off prematurely. They can be frustrated even further when they find that touch papers are dampened so that nothing goes quite to plan.
The male ego is a fragile thing and pranksters emerge when you least expect them.

The B-team have made excellent preparations, they are mostly ex-army themselves and though civilians now, the sort of blokes you can trust. They understand the need for accuracy, safety and communication. As I pass through, I can tell that they all know their jobs and what has to be done, by whom and when…all except one, whose always been a bit of a maverick and never could do as he was told, not even as a boy. As a man he should know better, but in truth he believes that he does know better, better than them all and has already decided what in actual fact he'll be doing tonight, which bears little resemblance to their supposedly shared vision. He is the weakest link.

The B-team have placed the explosives at the farthest end of the meadow, away from the bonfires and in the widest part where the crowd will not go and as far as they can tell, the wind is blowing away from the road and should continue to do so for the rest of the evening. So long as they stick to the plan, nothing will go wrong. But Maverick Man is on the loose and he's already half-inched some kerosene, with a cunning plan to create a ring of fire atop the golf course to get their attention and from whence he will be setting off some rather impressive bombs of his own. He justifies his plan to himself as being an ace entertainer and man of vision and having been made a legitimate member of the B-team, he obviously knows what he's about and is determined

17

to make it a night to remember, by using that extra element of surprise. What a plonker!

Lurking behind him on the golf course is our photographer, still looking for the things that others overlook and catching them in her camera, catching him in her camera is not what she intends to do, but catch him she does as she eventually captures what she's been hunting down all afternoon.

Both bonfires are lit at 6:00pm, early enough to light the way of friends and neighbours coming into the meadow. The crowd is settled, wrapped and feeding as the first fireworks are lit. There is an "ooh!" and an "aah!", and it's going rather well. I can pick up the buzz from many, as I pass through them, one head after another, between my natural place on The Path and across the huge and ever growing crowd in the lower meadow. Crow Man is there on the edge, he's had a wonderful day outdoors where he's happiest, gathering old wood and dragging it towards the pile ready for younger men to throw it aloft. Here he stands now, happy with a hot-dog and a nice cool beer. The bangs keep coming and it has a strange effect on me, like an echo of an ancient experience long forgotten. It is having a physical effect that is frankly discombobulating, but I keep my level and keep on moving, until the next one comes and the next, then unexpectedly, from the other side of the road, away from the main event,

18

there comes a blaze of unexpected light and a heat like a thousand suns, in starkest contrast to this damp and chilly night, followed by screams and the largest explosion I have experienced in a few centuries. The energy that hits me is extreme in itself and I fly up into the sky to 10,000 feet before I manage to pull myself to a halt and start to fly back down. As I descend I see a terrifying scene. Maverick Man is being chased by something determined and fiery; super-charged, yet will-o-the-wisp like. He is so terrified that he runs through the ring of fire that he's created, to get away, igniting fully just as he powers across the Ditchling Road into the stream of traffic, towards the meadow. The smoke that is now blowing from his golf-side blaze, as the relentless wind blows it across the road, is blinding the drivers to each others' whereabouts, masking the treacherous bends in the road and leading them into each other and down the bank into the wood.

The alarm is sounded and the three men are despatched to save the day. They have been expecting this, they have trained for this. No-one, but Lurking Photographer and I, sees the huge mist and fire-breathing apparition, that unexpectedly swoops into the fray, something ancient from a hidden world, not a will-o-the-wisp after all, drawing a huge surge of power from the instant and tangible fear emanating from the gathered crowd, as it chases Maverick Man, who is

19

screaming still...and she, Lurking Photographer, captures that which she has been waiting for all afternoon and evening, in her lens, but not quietly as she had anticipated. Where did that thing come from?

The summoned squad car races up the hill, vroom, vroom, vroom and turns the corner once, vroom, vroom, vroom and turns the corner twice, racing at top speed over familiar tarmac to the familiar but dangerous bend in the road. Coming to save the victims who have ploughed off the road and down into the wood, when suddenly all visibility is lost and the shock in that moment of the uncertainty ahead, causes that man, the third man who was not a wimp but the driver of the car, to have a heart attack at the wheel as they inevitably follow the other vehicles off the edge of the bend in the road and down, down, down into the wood as well.

Chapter 3: **Cause and Effect**

Nothing is the same after that night. The community is shaken, rattled and rolled, literally into a ditch in some cases, but amazingly nobody passed over. Nobody knew what happened to Maverick Man after he ran through the crowd aflame and out the other side, up to the top of the meadow, where his fellow B-teamers stood stunned, mouths gaping and watching in disbelief as he continued running all the way to the top, crossing the poignantly sad A27 flyover and into Stanmer Woods. Passing into legend, as he did so, as possibly the most stupid person ever to be given access to explosive material.

From my new position, which is now, for some unexplainable reason some 50 feet above The Path, I continued my patrol. Maybe it was a trust issue that had crept into my otherwise normally comfortable relationship with these familiar people of this small community, or maybe I had just fundamentally changed in the moment of the huge explosion. It awoke something buried deep within me. An echo of something past and coupled with the ferocious energy of the flaming apparition whose power still lingered around The Path, was preventing me from leaving and preventing me from settling. I felt discombobulated. An echo of a former time that I could not shake and did not want to either. A desire to get away and explore was growing and I could feel the vibration of it increasing in my very fabric every moment of the day and night as the days went on. Something still held me here in this place though, for now, as golden Autumn turned to white Winter and the magical allure of the sparkling snow mesmerised me and took its grip.

Chapter 4: **Winter**

In plummeting temperatures of down to minus 8, Winter's grip prevented many from walking, running or cycling The Path. There were those stalwarts with their spiky or springy crampons who would not be deterred and duly equipped, still able to stride The Path in a confident manner, but they were few and far between. It became a path unpeopled for the most part, leaving it to nature and its inevitable descent from Autumn, in all its waning glory, into Winter.

The winter winds coming off The Downs sculpted the snow into mini hills and troughs that took little account of the landscape that lay underneath. I knew the shape of things with ease, diving deep below the snow in order to explore the gritty landscape underneath, that I knew in finite detail. The sound of the road was properly muffled now, with the soft absorbing qualities that only snow brings and double muffled under the snow itself, though the road's vibrations were still there, deeply humming at the passing of every vehicle and persistently coming up through the ground. It was like another world under the snow, a world where small shrews and mice, could wander in relative warmth by comparison to the exposed world above, where the bitter wind stripped the heat out of everything and though illumination was dulled below the snow in comparison to the penetrating light above, it was still a somewhat magical and softly illuminated world, where light diffused through sufficiently to light their little ways.

Above the snow the world shone like a diamond, made more beautiful by the crystal clear blue sky against which the snow looked nothing short of perfect. The buzz it gave me caused me to reverberate at an even higher vibration than I had, since The Bang and without even trying at all, I was lifted back up to my now habitual 50 feet above it all. The blue and white that I could see was faintly reminiscent of another place I was now remembering, where blue and white blessed each other in the blazing hot heat of a Mediterranean sun instead. I want to see these places again, to re-acquaint myself with my past.

A murder of crows, as thick as the blackest night descends into the white landscape, surrounding Crow Man, who waits with his bag of scraps that will keep them rooted and living in this world at this bleakest time of year. They are grateful to him, this familiar and ancient man who is almost one of them too, all bar his lack of wings. The smaller birds had bushes crammed full with the brightest red berries and the shiny black sloe to keep them alive. They hopped from branch to branch and bush to bush, keeping busy, keeping warm, keeping something in their bellies to see them through until Spring. Their recent ancestors used to peck the foil tops off the milk bottles on doorsteps to survive, but the supermarket revolution put an end to that. The birds and I own this winter landscape, as the erstwhile users of The Path huddle in their houses waiting for Christmas to cheer them in the interim, but mostly waiting for Spring.

I focus on these birds and the small mammals that scurry from one side of The Path to the other, looking for something to eat, but not staying above the snow and exposed for too long. I don't feel the cold like they do, I am aware that it holds a different vibration, much shorter and higher pitched than the languid vibration that comes with the heat of a summer's day. The crows, the magpies and other carrion arrive like mobsters every time some poor beast meets its end on the road.

Today there is a mother fox, caught coming out of the wood across The Path, then the road, making a dash for the golf course in search of food round the back of the club house, by the bins. Her desperate hunger driving her to distraction, robbing her of her wits and resulting in her demise under the wheels of a Continuity Foods lorry as it makes it's way back towards town after a very long day of deliveries. I pass through the driver and feel her pain, which is genuine at the mistake made after such a very, very long day. Nobody should have to work these hours, she's thinking.

As I rise back up carrying the vibration of her pain within me, I realise that I am not the only witness to this scene, Lurking Photographer is here too, having returned to the site of Autumn's night of disaster, to explore the possibility that the powerful energy she captured in her lens still lurks, awaiting another such event or maybe just to reassure herself that the shape that she captured in her lens that night was for real. No surprise that such things might choose to remain around a site of such historic interest, just outside what would have been the flint walls of the Neolithic Hollingbury Hill Fort.

It's a rare treat to see her here again, so I pass through to ascertain what she is thinking and I can tell that she is both fearful and hopeful in equal measure. She seeks the truth and knows that her whole life has been leading her towards it, but as yet doesn't know what that might look like. She is brave.

Winter is lonely on The Path as I find that passing through small mammals gives me little food for thought, other than their thoughts about food. I am missing the plentiful Summertime's passing intellectuals and yearn for more fruitful opportunities. What am I doing here on this path in the middle of Winter?

My only hopes for company are the dog walkers, who stroll through the wood for some protection from the wind and bitter icy rain that has started to replace the incessant falling snow that we have had for almost 6 weeks. This rain is worse than the snow as it slices through woolly hats and gloves, coats, hair and insufficiently waterproofed shoes, to the blue skin beneath that will take hours to recover its colour on return to the house. Even passing through them is to be met with disappointment, as like the smaller mammals and birds, the thoughts I pick up all revolve around thoughts of survival in one form or another. Where is the joy? Where is the relaxed intellectualism, the luxury of wondering and planning that is typical of a nice warm mind? The cold makes people shrink, not think.

I am trapped by The Path and now resent my daily oscillations from one end of it to the other. Beginning of The Path, middle of The Path, end of The Path; end of The Path, middle of The Path, beginning of The Path...there had to be more than this filling my existence.
Crow Man is out and about as usual and my only solace, since he is a genuinely happy and generous soul whom I admire for his consistency and fortitude, there is no other

like him on The Path and the very length of his long and happy life and the memories that he re-lives as he wanders The Path and the fields that surround it, tell a tale of goodness and contentment that send out some of the highest vibrations I have felt on passing through. He is loved and he feels it every day, from his wife, his children and the many grandchildren in his life, but strangers do not see that about him, they assume that he is just eccentric and alone, but they could not be more wrong. This is a good man, living a good life with a capacity for joy like no-one else.

Chapter 5: **Spring**

The sap is starting to rise at last and The Path once again becomes the focus for local life. Tiny signs of growth and hope push forth every day from the seemingly devastated landscape. The banks of The Path are itching to pour forth the glory that has been stored up in locked-tight seed pods, some for many-a-year, husks cracked sufficiently this time by the harshest of winters since 1950, to allow them to sprout and flourish as soon as the damp and the warmth arrive in the exacting right proportions. Here comes Crow Man on his bicycle, which appears again each Spring and although I've seen it before, it's quite a sight for sore eyes, to see this slip of an ancient man find reserves of energy sufficient to propel him at such high and almost reckless speeds along The Path, sporting the biggest grin possible per inch of person. Spring is here!

You can see it in the step of Pale Physics Student, who is still pale, but must have continued his physical regime indoors throughout the winter, because he has bulked up a bit and looks ready to strut his newfound muscles up and down The Path with extra confidence, as these words fly from his lips, "Ich bin bereit, die Verantwortung für ein

Projekt von meinem eigenen zu nehmen", and from the look of him, I do believe that he is.

I have read his thoughts before, but somehow do not feel the need to dive in at all since he is exuding personal confidence and pushing out vibrations at a much higher frequency than ever before. Though actual joy does seem to be the missing piece of his personal puzzle.

Both Crow Man and Pale Physics Student had been there that night of the bonfire, when so much had gone wrong in so short a time. Luckily neither had been badly effected, though I am picking up on a determination in them both, post Winter, to live their lives to the full now that Spring is here and having passed through the traumas of Autumn and Winter in one piece.

Almost out of idle curiosity I pass through Crow Man and get a massive surge of positive energy that is almost like something singing at the highest pitch I've experienced since that single Sky Lark above the outer meadow last Summer; "I am alive and kicking and nothing's going to stop me, not wind, nor weather, nor my poor old bones, nor the speed at which I walk. Give me a new day, a bicycle and the wind in my hair and I'm the happiest man alive, indestructible!" ... as I pass through I feel some of this positivity stick to me and I carry it away with me, until I pass through Pale Physics Student, where I decide to drop it off.

Let's see what good that little piece of mischievous alchemy might do!

There is a new girl jogging The Path and I call her Froufrou, since that is exactly what she is, with her swishy ponytail hair and mouthy pout and a pony-like jog that always brought light sniggers and unexpected mild choking from other passing joggers. There is absolutely no understanding in Froufrou of how to jog or what jogging is in fact for, nor any desire to do anything other than mimic a My Little Pony, which I now know for sure since passing through. I feel a pang of guilt, since having passed on Crow Man's positivity to Pale Physics Student, so close to the passing of Froufrou on The Path and I summon all my energetic powers to keep him safe from colliding stupidly with her. The intention certainly was to fill the 'joy' gap in his world, but this young woman would not be capable of fulfilling that!

They pass on The Path and I can detect a rise in his hormone levels that sends a shiver through me, so I dive in, passing through, whilst creating the most almighty buzzing as I vibrate my very matter at the highest level I've managed to muster of late, which sufficiently distracts him until the danger passes.

31

There must be someone suitable on The Path, who shares his vision and drive.   The search is on.

Days pass one into another, with chilly winds and rain still terrorising the small beasts at night, but tiny bit by tiny bit, the temperature is rising alongside the sap and burgeoning life gets bolder and more plentiful.
Joy is suddenly all around, as boy-bird meets girl-bird and they do what birdies do…… and foxes scream long into the night at the side of The Path in the meadow, keeping the local residents awake. Dying cats and murdered children are among many of the speculations as to "what that noise might have been last night". I know, because I've watched them playing in the meadow grass.

Red-head treads The Path again, now that the warmth is returning and she meets the now shortened line of only two men coming the other way. They catch her eye and she smiles as her sensual fluidity gyrates enticingly, impossible to ignore. Sex on legs.

This warmer weather is really bringing them out. It's a much more interesting path now that Winter has been put to bed and the walkers, joggers and cyclists have returned, determined to cast off the winter layers of cloth and fat.

Another young man, but much younger than usual is next to take to The Path. He is taking this very seriously indeed, as he contemplates that The Path is for adults, which I know having passed through, and he actually believes that he is trespassing into their adult territory.

He cycled it once or twice under the protection of a parent, which legitimised its use then, but now, alone, he's almost frightened that he'll be challenged. Passing the shortened line of two men, he can tell that these guys are serious grown-ups, real men and he bows his head in an act of submission as they pass on The Path. Then coming up behind Red-head, he cannot help but wonder what a woman like that would do with a boy like him. I know that the answer is 'absolutely nothing at all'.

Moody Blonde joins The Path, jogging past this young man. I've seen her before, but not for almost a year. She's thinking the exact same thing as Red-head about the young man, as I pass through and pick up on the very much more focused and serious nature of her current thinking. Her time in Europe was wild and had allowed her to put off the boring bits of growing up, like having to study for her degree and saddle-bag the impressive weight of a student debt for what looked like an eternity. The thought of not going to University bothered her, since she had an excellent and enquiring mind, but had put it on ice for a while, which was beginning to weigh heavily too.

Balancing debt and a potentially unfulfilled life were the considerable thoughts crashing about in her mind this morning, so I pass on through yet again, to see what she is planning next. She's done the Love thing and she's done the hardening of the heart in order to save it from the inevitable disappointments and damage that badly behaved young men mete out, seemingly without a second thought.

Her next step was not yet University, since she was still very young in her year and felt a desire to establish her credentials as an independent and strong young woman, to be taken absolutely seriously in the world, before diving into an academic environment peopled largely by what she now considered to be 'the very young'. Her intention was to enter the world of academe when she could deliver some proper punches, be listened to and with a clear and steely determination about what she needed to get out of it. To be taken seriously by all, which frankly evades the blonde female in this society, however brilliant her mind.

Moody Blonde has really shaped up since she's been away, with a figure that would stun most men into silence and cause most women to get the claws out. She is also musing on the April Fools joke played on her a few days before and I see that she still lacks any confidence about her appearance that the prank brought to the fore, which I know when I pass through and this imbalance, I determine, needs addressing.

As I pass through again I can feel the longing to feel safe and to be loved, not for her immaculate curves, but for the brilliant mind that she keeps safe under that perfect flow of blonde. I rise up to ascertain the whereabouts of Pale Physics Student, for though he's pale, his mind is a match for hers and that would be an excellent result. There he is, about to leave The Path at the other end, so for today I content myself with delivering her latest thoughts into his head...'looking for love and wanting to make her mark'. There is an immediate and rousing interest created in him that I pick up...'if only I could find such a girl', so to make the seed-planting complete, I take that thought back from one end of The Path to the other and as I pass through for the last time, I leave that thought with her. I am enjoying passing thoughts from one soul to another as I pass through and find Spring's sap rising in my vibrational body too at the prospect of playing with this power and playing cupid as the weather warms up and the people of The Path come out to play.

Chapter 6: **Summer**

As Spring turns to Summer, the flowers are shouting out in their loudest voice as one, in an irrepressible riot of exquisite colour, sun-struck with happiness. The colour hits the eye of the users of The Path and penetrates their hearts, reminding them that life is good.
Moody Blonde has gotten into a great rhythm and hits The Path every day, fitting it in around her shifts at the pub and the clinic and though she is tired to her very core by everything that she is juggling in order to survive, she has a plan that keeps her going. I get a download of her plan as I pass through and it makes me sure that she too will go a long way in this world.

Something good is coming her way today and although it's taken over a month, I know what it is. Love is in the air and its vibration is already on The Path, heading her way. Whether they know it or not, these two were connected in the Spring when I passed through and through again, until they were irreversibly connected by that tiny thread of thought and a mutual longing for Love.
Ahead of her on The Path is Froufrou, doing her very finest My Little Pony impression and I panic momentarily when I realise that both girls are heading the same way, but I

needn't have worried since Moody Blonde is a proper runner and she leaves Froufrou prancing pointlessly behind in no more than the blink of an eye.

Crunch, crunch, crunch coming closer to the middle from the end of The Path, crunch, crunch, crunch coming closer to the middle from the beginning of The Path. The sun is high in the sky, this June day and they are both perspiring gently. From the distance they clock each other and an unexplainable moment of recognition hits each of them in the exact same nanosecond.

There is blushing and a welcome familiarity in the other energetic body that is heading their way, the power of which somehow takes control like a magnetic force driving them rapidly forward toward each other, or maybe they both just lose control at the same time, it's hard to tell as they inexplicably collide. Smash! Bang, ouch!, collapse…they both fall down on The Path onto their similarly fit behinds and then very quickly gather themselves as they sit up facing each other and instead of pouring out the expletives that Froufrou was expecting to hear as she caught up with the scene, they are laughing and smiling like the very best of friends. "They must know each other" she is thinking as I pass through her uncluttered mind. "I'm so sorry", "so am I", "No, please don't be", "It's my fault too, I have no idea what came over me", "me neither, but maybe we could talk about it over lunch?", did those words really just come out of his mouth? What a result, job done and I whizz off up to 100 feet, in celebration.

The Summer is so very fulfilling as I watch the riot of colour unfold anew every day. Blue cornflowers, vibrant red poppies and the last of the late primroses left over from Spring. Never before have there been so many poppies! That bitter Winter really did its job, cracking open every long forgotten seed and calling them all out of their deepest hiding places, to share their exquisite frail beauty with the world.

Moody Blonde and Pale Physics Student are in Love, that much is obvious and she is massively impressed by his vision that, on graduation, will take him to a Masters degree then on to Cern in Switzerland, since he has been encouraged to pursue a place as one of their future intake of Apprentices. This is my kind of man, she is thinking, as I pass through and I am energised at the thought that she can see that.

He cannot believe his luck, that being brainy has paid off so well for him. Not only has he been forecast a 1st in his Physics degree, but he has been given special recognition for having learned both technical French and German from a standing start and under his own steam, sufficiently good enough that he was able to conduct his recent Cern interview using them both fluidly alongside English. His parents are so very proud, and now, as if the Universe has decided that he really is some kind of a God, worthy of godly gifts and recognition, has sent him a beautiful, intelligent and funny Goddess with whom he would love to spend the rest of his days. But don't be fooled people, these two are not hopeless romantics, they are actually two of the most pragmatic young people I have had the pleasure to pass through and I can pick up that their individual ambitions far outweigh any momentary lovey-dovey stuff they might currently be enjoying, so they will enjoy each other whilst it suits them, and both have plans to take different paths in the coming few years, in order to maximise their potential for success and to pursue their individual visions.

Finals are looming for Pale Physics Student and he determines to use every joule of energy in achieving, so time with Moody Blonde is minimised, but all the more intense and pleasurable due to its rarity. Less is more.

This suits her well, since she is working every available hour in order to save sufficiently to travel the world wherever and however she chooses. Meeting him has confirmed her ultimate determination to study psychology and neuroscience, so that she can become a clinical psychologist, capable of deep-diving into the minds of others in order to help them live lives that fulfil their true potential.

The energetic buzz I receive when I pass through is huge, as I realise that she and I are like twins! So very similar in both our desire to understand people and our desire to make them happy and fulfilled whilst they are blessed with the gift of life.

I decide also that we are both rather nosey.

Chapter 7: **Relentless Repetition**

This path has been my home, my play-ground, my entertainment and my prison these past ten years and though there have been some more and some less fulfilling times, when the energy has seemingly leached away, the energy levels have also been so intense at times that I've almost exploded whilst trying to keep it all in.

The Autumn's events unsettled me and awakened something that I have since failed to accurately identify or pinpoint and also have absolutely failed to quash. Oscillating from one end of The Path to the other has given me some minor momentary purpose, a minute by minute or second by second goal from the point at which I find myself and the obvious objective at the other end, but with no obviously fulfilling end result on arrival. The lack of fulfilment and the sense of a lack of purpose has caused the tension to build up in my perfect little Atomic body. What is the point of it all?

Trying to focus on what it all means, a vibrational tension rises in my body, delivering the realisation that, in spite of my magnificent potential, I have somehow fallen into a very boring pattern that has dulled me to such an extent and disconnected this little Atom from the massive and inexhaustible vibration of an awesome, never ending and ever expanding Universe.

My disconnect is hard to accept yet almost total. Not only do I feel a low-level vibration akin to sadness, more frighteningly I can feel an intense vibration growing in my very core which can only be described as being a rather ferocious, irrational and dangerous anger.

This little Atom has to leave this place, or I fear that I'll unwittingly create a type of 'hell-on-earth' in this sleepy little part of Sussex. So I leave.

(Middle) The middle is a huge and bounteous landscape in which our life and youth allows us to explore.

Chapter 8: **Going off-piste**

Up, up, up my little Atomic self soars, neither knowing nor caring whither or thither. Nobody will miss me since they couldn't see me even whilst I was around, not even with the most powerful microscope in the Physics department at Sussex.

I do quietly believe that they had felt my presence at times and that their lives would have been the poorer had I not chosen to spend a decade adoring those people, in that sleepy little part of Southern England.

Once on my ascent up through the water-vapour-filled lower part of Earth's atmosphere, I pass through all of the birds and aeroplanes as they present themselves. Wet-clouds and ice-clouds, snow-clouds and electric storm-clouds all present themselves too, as I zoom up in a perfectly perpendicular line, straight up from the point on The Path from which I launched myself. I take stock of how it feels vibrationally and realise that in passing through it all, I have detected a menu of gases whose molecules are vital for sustaining life on this beautiful planet. This 'knowing' disturbs me, since it represents the issues that this planet is facing. Earth would be nothing without common nitrogen, oxygen and many of the somewhat more magical things that man has discovered for his own frivolous entertainment. Life, enhanced and made possible by the existence of argon, neon, helium, methane, carbon dioxide, krypton, hydrogen, xenon, ozone, nitrous oxide, carbon monoxide, ammonia and iodine molecules that I have just bathed in.

I remember leaving The Path to hear that portly Irish Comedian, who played the Brighton Dome last year, whose whole set was about the global shortage of liquid helium, because it has been mis-used and over-used to create a raised vocal vibration, for 'a bit of a laugh'.
Such a rare gas, used to cool down the superconductive magnetic coil in all MRI scanners to a temperature below 10 Kelvin, so that it can be used to diagnose rare diseases and without which, the saving of such lives would be rendered impossible. Yet the feckless folk of planet Earth, agreed that having a quick laugh at someone sounding a bit like Donald Duck, was somehow more important. I liked that Comedian, with his incisive intelligence and his ability to drive the message home. He'd make an excellent Prime Minister I

muse in that moment. Maybe I will arrange that, if I ever come back this way.

I am beginning to re-awaken on leaving Earth and can feel my vibration zinging more lightly with joy and delight at this taste of the potential to re-discover things past and also to remember things long ago forgotten.

Earth's atmosphere, I know, is one of the reasons why life can survive on this special planet and compared to many planets that I have visited, this is quite a thick atmosphere that has created a nurturing blanket, engulfing it like the warm and generous love of a fabulous mother.

As I soar higher still, I find myself passing out of the troposphere, through the tropopause buffer zone, into the thinner air of the stratosphere, where the air flow is mostly horizontal and it carries me immediately sideways out over Southern Ireland and into the stratospheric air above the North Sea. Higher still I rise, engaging my Will this time, to see just how far I can go. I am shaking inside, at such a high vibration now with an energy created out of absolute excitement I suspect, that I almost don't notice the change in atmospheric composition, but it has changed. I know for sure that I am passing through a layer of tremendous importance, a layer that has spent millennia protecting this verdant planet from the ultraviolet radiation emanating

45

from The Sun. Protecting the green of this planet from destruction.

A layer only created itself by the very green that's producing the oxygen required to achieve this. A symbiotic relationship with a level of co-dependence so fragile, that a minor fall-out between these two will spell the end of life on Earth.

It is patchy and inconsistent this protector of the planet, this Ozone Layer, doing its level best, but seemingly losing the battle that it's so stoically fighting. In this atmosphere of gases that envelop this little planet Earth, I know what the problems are, since I have done some analysis, measuring the relative quantities of gases right the way up to where I passed through the ever-thinning Ozone and out into dark space, on my way to visit beautiful Venus.

Above the stratosphere is the mesosphere and above that is the ionosphere, where I acquire a colossal electrical charge as I pass through it, that is like a turbo-charging of what was already becoming a not inconsiderable energetic potential. I glory in the situation as I am surrounded by the most beautiful light show that I have encountered in many an Aeon.

The aurora is all around me and it bursts softly, yet powerfully across the ionosphere, chucking electrically charged colour into atmospheric pockets, like the throwing

46

of that coloured powder that I witnessed at the Hindu Holi festivals in India across many decades, celebrating Spring and Love on the full moon of the Vernal Equinox.

Simultaneously, I am hit by the sounds of a thousand voices singing, talking, chatting, laughing, where the radio shows of the world unite in a cacophony of communication. Isn't that Opus 17?; Frankie Vali & the Four Seasons?; The One Show?; Sarah Cox and Steve Wright? Deep joy.

I feel buzzy and dizzy, as I pass through this confused pocket of sound, with the joy and energy that they bring and as they combine, this rises within me powerfully and irrepressibly.
Nothing can stop me now as I burst forth, like an Atomic orgasm, out into deepest space.

Chapter 9: **Beautiful Venus**

It's a long way to Venus from Earth, 26.9 million miles on this particular day in Earth's late Summer, to be exact. Venus will be beautiful, I tell myself as I pass through the endless night of deep space. She is waiting for me, with the lights on, to once again show me her treasures and re-kindle our romance.

I have seen them before, the last time I passed through and lingered long as I fell in love with her. I keep myself warm in deep space, from the vibrations that the knowledge of this old love is generating. Love, I have noticed on passing through it, has the capacity to raise the vibration of most every situation.

My sense of gratitude is so immense that I muse that if I were a human, I would have a gratitude jar like the one I saw in Moody Blonde's mind when I once passed through, that I would drop slips of paper into every time something special or magical happened along my way. It would be mighty full by now. The slip that I would add today would say 'I am grateful for being reminded, that I am a predominant and powerful force of nature. Indestructible and free to choose what I do and when I do it. Capable of

focusing on any result of my choosing and by engaging my
Will, achieving whatever it is, every time'.
Cogito, ergo, sum.

I'm coming to kiss you Venus and hoping that you remember
me, though it's more than two billion years since last we
met. I left you then, one petulant moment when your temper
started to fray, to visit your twin the Earth and to see
whether I could live without you. Earth had welcomed me
with open arms all those years ago and let me nestle and
play there, on and off, without judgement.
I came and went as I pleased. No questions asked as to
where I had come from and generously it allowed me access
to the depths of the deepest and richest oceans and the
heights of the freshest mountain tops, with magnificent
views across continents and lush depths in the wettest and
most verdant rain forests.
  YOU had cast me out.

As I speed across the Universe, I remember more clearly,
the last time that we met and that I had been expelled,
banished forever by you venting your anger and frustration,
seemingly without cause. I did not miss your hot temper,
these past two billenia, that started in those latter years.
That short fuse of yours, that ignited when you unthinkingly
let your atmosphere start to escape. But now I am coming

home to you, hoping that we can re-kindle our love and that you might have passed through your planetary menopause and re-balanced yourself back onto an even keel. I will regale you with tales of Earth, her beauty and richness, but also be sure to tell you that my love for you is all the greater, for having been away.

Absence makes the heart grow fonder.

26.9 million miles is a long way to travel for a promise of love, even for a highly energised and mighty Atom and it takes the best part of a day to get there, traveling faster than the speed of light. Approaching Venus, it's obvious that she isn't expecting me. The lights are off and nobody's home.

As I enter her upper atmosphere, I am hit by high velocity winds that grab me viciously and whisk me around that upper atmosphere faster than I can remember experiencing here before, so in order to escape them and regain some control, I push on down and pass through the cloud deck about 31 miles above the surface, which I realise, to my surprise is composed mainly of sulphuric acid and a zillion other corrosive compounds that are trying to eat into my perfect little outer coat.

I hurry on down through it, in order to escape the discomfort, only to find that I am passing through into an oppressively stagnant atmosphere where the winds are suddenly very weak indeed and in surprising contrast to that which I had just experienced above. I am thrown by the sudden change and almost collapse out of the sky, being so taken by surprise at the lack of resistance and I am left tumbling down towards the surface.

As I pass through I know for sure that she has changed beyond recognition, her atmosphere at the surface, is composed of about 96% carbon dioxide, with most of the remainder being nitrogen and where, oh where has all the water gone?
The next shock to my little atomic self, is the realisation that I am under a huge and unexpected amount of pressure, about 90 times that of the Earth's surface, that would instantly crush the life out of any and all of the exquisitely beautiful and perfectly formed birds and beasts that live so happily on Earth. This realisation is compounded by my picking up on the fact that, as I touch the surface of this now barren planet, that her surface is almost 930 degrees fahrenheit and she's gone and melted absolutely everything!

Her atmosphere had once been perfectly equipped to support life, but I know, as I pass through, that there is a mechanism in the Venusian atmosphere that has caused her to, very effectively, trap solar radiation.

I also know, as I pass through that this ability to trap solar radiation has been brought about as a direct consequence of a runaway greenhouse effect. Venus is not a generous mother like her twin the Earth, instead she is angry and rather than nurture, she's murdered everything, strangling the last breath out of the primordial soup that would have otherwise spawned life, such as I had found flourishing so beautifully on Earth and had seen the start of here too, 2 billion years ago.

Nothing from Earth could survive here and I do not wish to stay knowing that this is possibly Earth's fate if nothing is done to save the Ozone layer and keep out the solar radiation.

Without so much as a "hello" or "goodbye", I head straight on up, up, up and away. Away from this Evil twin of Earth's, where oceans have evaporated and all life has been crushed, trying my level best to swallow my massive disappointment and hoping that there's somewhere else in the Universe, that I might find solace.

Chapter 10: **Maybe Mars?**

At first, once I have freed myself from Venus, I wander pointlessly about wondering why nothing stays the same any more, convinced that it never used to be So. Feeling unable to return to Earth so soon, I decide that before any return is possible, that I need to find an interim destination.

I fear that I might be met once again with a crushing disappointment if I were to return to some other planet that I had previously enjoyed. That would not do very much to raise my catastrophically reduced vibrational levels and so I choose to visit masculine Mars instead, since it purports to be the antithesis of Venus. The decision, once made, causes my energy levels to return. I have no idea what I will find, which gets the vibration up further still.

The average distance from Venus to Mars is 9.80 astronomical units, or 74,364,646 miles and since planets are forever moving about, a distance that there is no real way of being certain how long that might take me to span, so I decide not to concern myself with such things and just set a course that focuses on the end result of being on Mars in time to see 'something spectacular'. I'm pleased to be able to report that that is exactly what happened.

Mars sits in the same solar system as my beloved planet Earth and so I do not feel that I am straying too far from where I now realise that I have left my little Atomic heart. As I travel towards it, I can see that there are two small moons orbiting Mars that look very much like a couple of Earthly spuds, that would be happier cloaked in dark soil than in this thin and predominantly nutrient-free atmosphere through which I pass.

The first that I encounter is Phobos, a dusty little potato of a planet, heavily cratered and streaked with grooves, though larger than its brother Deimos whom I can also see a little farther off looking smaller and wonkier, but shining as brightly as Venus does, though definitely no less dusty than its brother.

I know from my many 'passings' through the mind of Pale Physics Student, that there is a mission called PADME planned to Phobos & Mars, which should be completed by 2021 and that he has every intention of being on that team, sitting in one of the more important seats at mission control. Neither of these moons of Mars has an atmosphere, which I ascertain as I pass through and also that their gravities are far too slight to retain one. Deimos' two largest craters are charmingly named after Earth's 19th Century writers, Swift and Voltaire. Earthlings' penchant for the anthropomorphism of everything that they encounter, it occurs to me, is an excellent demonstration of their innate need to conquer and to feel at home. Be it countries or planets, everywhere they go, they leave their mark.

I can see that the future for these two moons does not look good, with every likelihood that they will meet their ends drawn in by gravity and smashed onto the surface of the Martian landscape, like a couple of mashed spuds. I learn, as I pass through its atmosphere, that Martian surface gravity is only 37% of the gravity to be found on Earth, meaning that any Earthling visitors could leap three times higher here, than they could back home. I speculate about a possible future Martian Olympics should this planet be populated and how very impressive those High-jumpers records would look.

Leaving its Moons far behind, I pass through the Martian atmosphere heading for the surface, which is made up of a stunning 96% CO_2. Future visitors from Earth will not be able to breathe Martian air since it is mostly carbon dioxide, with only a few traces of nitrogen, oxygen and water vapour. I float about demonstrating little control, unless I really engage my will, in this incredibly thin air, with an atmospheric pressure 100 times less than that of Earth.

As if this was not bad enough, the temperatures on Mars at midday are never more than 20 degrees C and can fall as far as -153 in a Polar Winter.
As I pass through, I pick up that Mars has changed over time, from being a much warmer, wetter and habitable planet, with a thicker atmosphere, which at some point and for some unexplained reason, started to leak away into space, forcing its surface water to disappear.

This tale of climate change is sounding rather familiar now and I wonder why I have traveled so far just to find this out, but I have to stay in order to learn all that I can, since it occurs to me that I now have a special gift to bestow, that will enable me to share some of this wisdom with my favourite Physicist, on my return to Earth.

As I work my way around the planet, to see what I can see, I fix upon a huge structure, that I learn as I pass over it, to be the tallest mountain in the Solar System, Olympus Mons. Now that is something spectacular! Not a mountain at all, but actually a volcano over 21 kms high and 600 kms across and despite having been formed over billions of years, still seemingly flowing its lava about and as active as it ever was.

I head on down to its surface to take a closer look and detect a rise in temperature at the surface that would indicate that my hunch was correct. I can also see the inordinate amount of dust that is flowing fluidly, moving as if it were water, about the surface and know as I pass through it, that Mars delights in whipping up a storm that can sometimes last in excess of 3 months with ease. Though there is life of sorts on this Earth-neighbouring planet, I am already feeling a longing to return to the beauty of my old friend and mother, to enjoy it for as long as possible, before it joins these others whose best years are very far behind them.

Mars does have its charms though, this planet of hot, red dust storms and polar opposite temperatures, designed to confuse and test. Its year being almost twice that of Earth, means that a long Summer or a long Winter on Mars, are very long indeed, but conversely, depending on where The Sun is in its orbit, there can be more intensely challenging highs and lows of temperature, in much shorter seasons, designed to destroy.

As I pass through the dusty covering of the surface of Mars, I detect familiar materials, that I have encountered before on Earth and I know, as I pass through, that these tiny particles of the Martian atmosphere were from meteorites that had been violently ejected by Mars, only to float about

in the solar system as space debris for millennia, before
eventually crash-landing on Earth.

The Scientific community of Earth knows a lot more about
Mars than they like to let on. I knew this before I arrived
and I know it with ever more certainty now, as I pass
through.

As I pass across the surface of the planet and reach the
dark-side of the planet, that is now grappling with a
Martian Winter, I detect ice, which means that there is
water on this planet and I know, as I pass through that
there once was abundant life, though I can barely detect
anything now that I could describe as flourishing. Some
water still flows, even in this Winter and I know as I pass
through, that this is due to an intense quantity of salt,
which I also now know has had a lot to do with bringing the
previously abundant life on Mars, to a very saline end.

The Martian dichotomy is in its contrasting landscapes, with
its rugged southern half consisting of craters and highlands
and the north with its smooth basins, dry lake beds and
sinuous dry riverbeds, both capped off with icy poles, that
grow and shrink with the changing seasons.

Seasonal change is inevitable, but the real sadness lies in
what it has lost. There is true beauty in the red of this
planet and some strength too, and I know from passing

through, that this is from the dust and rock being so very rich in iron. This planet is an Iron Man indeed!

I know, as I pass through the very core of this planet that it has a solid Iron heart doing its best to keep what little atmosphere it has, by creating a barely sufficient and weak magnetic pull. There is something rather tragi-romantic about this situation on Mars, a rather hopeless tale of loss. Losing all the battles that the ancient Greeks and Romans had imagined this warring planet winning. Down on his luck after the breakdown of a celestial love affair, maybe with that fickle Venus?

I am almost ready to leave Mars, with my vibration somewhat dulled by the deadly realisation that it's a gonner, in terms of any speculation that humans might possibly flee here in case of real trouble on Earth. So I take another swoop around the surface, picking up on some new areas, including some very chaotic terrain that I know to be called the Noctis Labyrinthus, or the Labyrinth of the Night, a region where two tectonic plates meet and have smashed each other up mightily over the millennia, causing a catastrophic collapse of the surface into a maze of deep troughs, pits and canyons. My journey through these reveals the disturbing truth that the harshness of the heat and the extreme cold has destroyed the substrate and will continue to hollow out this labyrinth, until it cuts a swathe through the whole planet.

Mars has no future.

I pull my mighty atomic self away from this hopeless case and taking the long route home, head back to Earth, where I can still see some hope yet, if only the right messages can be delivered into the right heads.

Chapter 11: **The Laws of Thermodynamics**

As I travel through Space, I contemplate the reception that I am hoping to get on my return to Mother Earth.

Should I head for Sussex and say "hi" to old friends, or whizz about the globe first, just to remind myself what an abundant and beautiful place she truly is? No matter. Anywhere on Earth knocks the spots off both Venus and Mars.

If only they could have been as well connected with each other as Moody Blonde and Pale Physics student were and with such little encouragement, they might have stood a better chance of survival. Communication is often the key. I rather like the little triangle that I have created between those two and this mighty Atom, which brings to mind the Zeroth Law of Thermodynamics: If two thermodynamic systems are each in thermal equilibrium with a third, then they are in thermal equilibrium with each other.

I was drawn to them both individually, from the get go, which doubtless led to the ease with which I managed to connect them to each other. This has to be the best Love Triangle ever created, but one I suspect, that I will be the only one to either identify as such or appreciate, since nobody else even knows of my existence. I reflect that I have developed rather a penchant for tragi-romantic thoughts of my own, since my visit to Venus and Mars and resolve to properly deal with this flaw in my make up at the earliest opportunity.

Trying to fathom how two such, once thriving, planets could fall apart to such a huge extent, I consider what might have in reality happened to the sufficiently good conditions that had once nurtured life and had since dissipated allowing it to go so very bad. If the first Law of Thermodynamics is to be believed, then: Energy can neither be created nor destroyed. It can only change forms. Through any process, the total energy of the Universe remains the same. Therefore, the life that had existed on both of these hopeless planets must in essence still be there or at least somewhere in another form. I have to accept that some chunks of both planets have been thrown off, as I know for certain that chunks of Mars have made it to Earth and who knows where bits of Venus might have ended up over such a lengthy passage of time!

The changes that have taken place, from being once vibrant living ecosystems, to the now dying or dead and seemingly useless matter that they have become, might take account of the energetic value that they represent from beginning to end, but what is not clear, is what actually happened in the middle to burn it all up and send bits of it flying off into space.

Without a reliable witness, it's impossible to tell and therefore impossible to know with any certainty how to prevent history from repeating itself elsewhere.
I can only surmise, that the First Law of Thermodynamics can do little to prevent the cycle of global warming from laying Earth to waste, since that particular Law is almost guaranteeing that it will happen!

But this story is not about the Laws of Physics, but moreover about Love, which is where I now turn my attention, as I ponder the possibility that Pale Physics student and Moody Blonde might have found it. I just hoped that if I ever caught up with the two of them again, that I would find that the sum of the two of them together had become greater than the sum of their individual parts. That Love had grown and that Love, like energy, was lasting.

Chapter 12: **Reaching Absolute Zero in Australia**

Re-entering Earth's atmosphere, below me, I see a vast and dusty landscape, that I soon know, as I pass through it, to be the Great Victoria Desert of Central Australia. I can see that it almost dissects this vast continent in two as it cuts a swathe from West to East.

As I pass through the pebbly and sandy surface, I pick up on traces of Plutonium-239 radioactive contamination, that I know to be left over from nuclear weapons tests carried out by the British in the 1950s and 60s. I decide not to hang around since that stuff is seriously bad for you. I am aware that if I pick any of it up, I might pass it on, when I pass through someone or something, with potentially catastrophic health impacts for them down the line.

Instead I rise up once more, above the very minimal layer of water vapor that has formed the thinnest of whispy clouds in the early morning air, in search of something more positive to explore today. I cannot bear to dwell on thoughts of destruction. I head for the very centre of this vast continent and find a huge red rock jutting out of the landscape and sitting slap bang right in the geographical middle. I learn that this is Uluru as I pass through and can hear the voices of the Aboriginal ancestors, who's land this is and who are keeping a watchful eye on things still.

From above I can see that it sits in the middle of a desert and yet still has a verdant water-hole at its summit, that has sustained life here for millennia. Uluru looks like it has been thoughtfully placed, yet most clumsily sculpted, by a clever giant, out of a mixture of red clay and red-stained papier mâché. Here it sits completely unique and alone, apart from the Anangu Aboriginal people and the Spirits of the Ancestors who keep faith with the ancient traditions on majestic Uluru in the magical middle of nowhere.

As I pass through this vast red rock, it reminds me a little of Mars and my spirits lift as I swear that it is faintly humming a familiar tune by that English singer Jeff Beck, "I'm everywhere and nowhere baby, that's where I'm at, going down a bumpy hillside, in your hippy hat", I know that the lyrics are being mis-quoted by these mischievous Ancestors, when I pass through, but it's certainly an apt and playful reminder of what's been happening in my world of late.
Uluru, it seems, can see me and also has a sense of humour. I land on the red rock, to connect with its deepest and most ancient vibration, oh and to catch the end of the song. To

this day, I truly do not recall what happened next, but suspect that I relaxed just a little whilst singing along to the tune and had also worn myself out to such an extent, with all the travels and the traumas, that I must have allowed my little vibrating body to give in to it. I fell a very long way into the deepest slumber as I landed. I fell all the way down from Mars as I let go of my connection to it and my vibration level hit absolute Zero.

I know now, on coming back to consciousness on this earthly plane, that I slept for almost an Earth calendar year. That year was full of dreams of journeys and journeys pursuing dreams, which took me back across time and space to the very dawn of time, when everything started with the splitting of a single Atom, blasting everything into being. Was that Atom me, or was that some much mightier Atom? If it split, then I am surely just one of its parts?
I have no idea what the answer to these questions is, as I drifted in and out of my vibrating body, as if I had been taken by a mighty fever.
There was pleasure in this letting go and I felt safe re-living old memories of what had already been, since I knew what those outcomes were and the past could not threaten the now, nor be changed. My deepest fears all came from what the future holds for this planet and I just wished that I could have connected with that, by way of some magical visionary

foresight or absolute wisdom, so that I would be sufficiently informed to deliver the truth and in sufficient time, when I eventually pass through the minds of the powerful of this planet. Like a Shaman journey I walked a path in my imagination, guided by my tiny atomic heart, slightly heady and delirious, a mixture of euphoria and a mild illness. It lifted me out of time and space and onto a seemingly endless path where I could see everything from a new perspective as I walked it back in time. I walked this path backwards through eternity, retracing my journey and seeing everything that I had ever seen, since time began. I headed back until I saw the birth of the Universe 13.7 billion years ago, when the Big Bang went off and there was inflationary expansion accompanied by unimaginable temperatures, that have been slowly cooling, to this time of liveable perfection, ever since.

The power that I acquired on this journey seemed to feed my very core, drawing the energy out from the creation of everything that had ever been made and storing traces of it inside me. I know, by passing through the history of time and space and reconnecting with these experiences, that I am storing their power and etching them once again into my atomic interior, so that I can draw upon them when they are needed the most.

When I awake, I am not inclined to leave Uluru straight away, even after so long here sleeping, as this place of safety and comfort has also proved itself to be a necessary place for reflection, before taking the next important step on my journey.

Having heard about the power of meditation and having felt so empowered by the dreaming, I spend the rest of the year in the warmth of the Australian sun, avoiding the winter of the northern hemisphere and connecting everything back up again in order to know what step was the next best one to take. Hurling myself off across the Universe, in my imagination, I am aware that I have the power to take that virtual journey whenever I please and for it to be as powerful as an actual journey and much more influential than I could have believed possible.
Now the deepest of deeply nourished, with my atomic batteries fully charged, I go in search of beauty, abundant life and people.

Heading global South, I hit the top of the country and find that I am flying in over a banana plantation, in the region of what I learn to be Cairns, as I pass through, where I can see about 20 young people gathered here from all over the world, working harmoniously in and around the tall banana palms. They are singing songs and telling jokes, as they disconnect

68

the huge hands of bananas from the tall palms and shoulder them across to the waiting diesel truck. The occasional spider loses its footing and drops out as they are hoisted up and over shoulders and into the back of the vehicle. Nobody seems to notice, or to be particularly bothered by these insects, even though I know, as I pass through that these 'banana spiders' are Brazilian Wandering Spiders mostly, that would happily kill anyone that they could get their fangs into. The Banana palms are growing in wide, organised rows, so that the truck can pass through, driven by one of the young crew. There is no lack of space here, so no need to cram things in, which makes for a much more pleasant working environment. There is a charm to the scene which I gladly observe all day, because the chopping and the humping is faintly reminiscent of how things were done centuries ago all over the planet, though then, with a non-polluting wooden cart and I know this, because I had been there to witness.

There is a tall boy working in a tailored but slightly scruffy suit jacket, welly boots and shorts, with dirty blonde hair and a shaggy beard. He has been there for some months now and is well liked by his fellow Banana Humpers. The pay is terrible, I read in his mind as I pass through, but also now know that he is only doing this to secure his visa, so that he can remain in this country for a year or so, in the warmth of the Australian sun and as far away from his Sussex home as he can get. He's a Sussex boy, I muse and feel an immediate connection. If it were warmer out in space, I suspect that he would have found a way to get there too, but he's contented himself with the simplicity of this set-up, as he prefers the honesty and integrity of this, to the modern world he's left behind. He's never been one for technology, nor needing lots of money, just a handsome boy with a huge capacity for love and a very good heart indeed.

I pass through again to see what else he is thinking and I know that though he is, so far, happy in his traveling adventures, that he has been traveling for well over a year looking for adventure and also looking for love. He has been across India, and many other places besides, where alone he faced packs of wild dogs hunting in the night and alone he climbed up huge mountain ranges in search of the best views and answers to those really big questions. He has met some wonderful, helpful people, but nowhere has he found that special someone and now, after more than a year of travel, he is feeling quite lonely. He misses his little sister and his mother, in particular.

He wished every day that some stunningly beautiful and exotic young woman would walk into his life, maybe even working on this farm in the humblest of situations, who could meet him and more to the point, match him. But the few that had passed through had not stayed long and none had been that exceptional. The girls back home, he was thinking, had always been such a disappointment. Rather more focused on the make and model of car that a young man drove, than the driving passions of his heart. He was all heart these days, this King of the Banana plantation. He worked hard and certainly had delivered value for very little money as a Banana Humper in Cairns. He had only a few weeks left to complete the governments stipulated time for working the land, so that he could get a visa that would allow him to remain for a year, working wherever he pleased. He planned to travel the coast, when he left here, on his way to Melbourne where he could re-engage with civilization and meet up with friends he'd met earlier in his travels.

On the day of my arrival, he has worked hard, as he always did and at the end of the day the youngsters gathered on a very long bench at the edge of the paddock, as they always did, where they would have a beer and regale each other with their usual teasings and telling the very best tales of the day, as they always did. Beer in hand, the King of Hearts describes the moment that he, in search of his lunch, had put his hand into the backpack at his feet, only to feel an unusually lively sandwich slide against his fingers. Leaping up and screaming a hundred curses, he had then

71

shaken the backpack upside down, only to see a deadly snake fall to the ground and slide malevolently away into the palms. "Had that bitten me, I'd be fucking dead tonight", he was saying " and you'd all be crying into your beers!", "yeah!" said a tall boy "and there'd be no-one to sing us shit songs tonight!". Followed by a roar of approval from the whole row.

They loved his songs and his guitar playing, which he'd perfected on his travels, by picking up every guitar he came across and giving it an evening of his undivided attention.

Now, I know from passing through this land, that Australia is home to 9 out of the 10 deadliest snakes on planet Earth and I also know, as I pass through, that the one that almost killed this King of Hearts was a Northern Crowned Snake, or Cacophis Churchilli and having lost its way had decided to hide in the nice shelter of the King of Hearts' bag. He was unlikely to have bitten him, that frightened snake, whose thoughts were on escaping the grabbing hand, but King of Hearts didn't know that and also, you really can never be too sure with snakes.

This light hearted and well-intentioned banter continued for a little while, until they saw the evening mini-bus coming up the track towards them, which always meant supplies and sometimes meant new recruits. King of Hearts was less interested these days, since he knew that he was leaving the farm in two weeks and heading for the city where he suspected he would meet a very special girl indeed, but they all stayed in line on the bench, like a welcoming committee of old men, in order to get a better view when the new recruits came towards them up the path. Squinting to get a better look, they could see that inside the bus there were girls!

Since he had been there, the boys had always out-numbered the girls by about 10-1 and this particular week there were no girls on the farm at all, but here came the magic bus to unexpectedly redress the balance.

The bus driver pulled the bus into the yard and jumped out, with unusual enthusiasm, to open the sliding side door of the mini-bus revealing a dark-haired boy with amazingly white teeth, who jumped down and then turned to help a stunning brunette off the bus first.

She too had a fabulous smile and jumped down shouting "hi" in an excited and rather high-pitched voice. 'Nerves', they were all thinking, as I passed through.

She was followed by an exotic dark-haired beauty, the like of which the Banana King had never seen before and I know, because I passed through both their heads within a millisecond, that it was mutual love at first sight. I passed through again quickly to pick up on their thinking and she was so excited to see what she knew to be the man of her dreams that she was fluttering inside like a Monarch butterfly with nervous excitement and a tinge of fear that was telling her that he might not see her...and he was immediately on fire the instant he saw her and determined that nobody else was going to even get a first word in with this beauty before he did, but had no idea how to make sure that it would be him that did.

So I passed each of their thoughts onto the other in turn and with that, she sailed confidently towards him in a sudden flare of sunlight, like some sky fallen beauty just landed from heaven and in one seamless movement, he stretched out his hand and she took it, joining him immediately and neatly on the bench at his side, with a friendly "hello", and where they both remained, completely contented, for the rest of the night. They talked all night like old friends and all of the next day and the King of Hearts could not believe that he had traveled all the way across the planet from Sussex, to find the love of his life, who, in turn and hot on his heels, had traveled all the way from Hampshire, to do the same. Not 50 miles between them at home and yet they had made this massive journey, as if to demonstrate to the Universe that they knew that this special person was really worth such a huge journey and that their love was worthy of its blessing. His fellow banana humpers had all noted that immediate and energetic connection between the two and none would have tried to muscle in on such an obviously perfect connection. They all loved the Banana King and were genuinely happy that he had, at last, found someone worthy of his attention.

Australia had filled me up. I had connected with the Ancient Ancestors of this land and they had blessed me by reconnecting me with myself, Love, Life and Sussex. It was time to continue my globetrotting, walking my current path to satisfy my curiosity before I returned to Sussex to see how it had managed without me. My plan was to take a journey home via the Americas, a circuitous route to see what I could see before heading back to England.

Something powerfully energetic was drawing me to these places as though they were pieces in a jigsaw puzzle that would each add to my understanding of the bigger picture that was trying to reveal itself to me, so I knew that I had to follow in order to connect up a few more of the many loose threads of my long life and to guide me on into the future.

Chapter 13: **I know the Truth**

What a neat little journey that proved to be, compared to the time taken to cross the Universe to visit Venus and Mars. The journey to the Americas felt like the equivalent of popping from one shop on a high street to the next. As I flew in over Albuquerque, I could see that it was not far from a gentle and welcoming town called Santa Fe, nestling in the New Mexico desert and which I knew as I passed through, to be the State capital. The energy here is best described as largely positive but unresolved. It has issues.

These people are genuinely happy in this place and welcomed the visitors that came through regardless of the time of year. The indigenous people, who lived in the Pueblos on the outskirts of the main town, wove fabrics and made beautiful silver and turquoise jewellery, mostly depicting Eagle feathers and ziggurat-patterned geometry. The symbols linked them to their ancestral roots, the raw materials dug from deep in the ground and that spoke of a glorious past where they were linked to a much higher ancient vibration than they could manifest these days. Craftspeople, highly skilled but somehow trapped and typecast by a governments' somewhat blinkered vision of how they might choose to live their lives in the modern world, which, as I pass through, now know has led to a huge amount of local frustration and resentment.

The disempowerment has led to deep personal disappointments too. Encouraged to live on the Pueblos to keep their ancient culture alive and fuelled by substantial guilt-fed government subsidies which had robbed them of their natural independence, encouraging them to stop innovating and squashing their chances of developing an evolved modern culture and creating a good many social problems as well.

The beauty and the craftsmanship in the silver work was reverberating at a very high vibration indeed and I understood why so many people who visited this place, left with at least one of these pieces in their possession.

Just outside Santa Fe and high above Albuquerque, I found an unusual little town, that was not really a town at all, but moreover a scientific research facility that I knew, as I passed through, had once been operated at a permanent state of red alert and the highest level of high security. Not so very long ago, you could neither enter or drive through this 'town', unless you had that top level security clearance, but in recent decades, since the cold war had ended and the United States of America had entered a time of entente cordiale with Russia, this little scientific research community at Los Alamos had relaxed its borders and now allowed most people to drive through and even shop, eat, bank or use the Laundromat. It had what I can only describe as a strange energy about it, that was at odds with its façade of normality. This town was hiding a huge secret or two, which I knew for sure, as I passed through.

One secret, I knew, was that there were things buried just outside town, that nobody could see but me. But then I could see everything and by passing through, I could know everything too and I was gaining ground in the absolute knowledge that there are no secrets from me once I've bothered to look. I had, or would soon have sufficient knowledge to be truly powerful.
Watch out world, I am thinking, don't mess with me, I am coming, choc full of knowledge and choc full of power and planning to put the 'wrong' things right!

This place is wrong. It is largely wrong because of its recent history of testing nuclear devises out in the desert in Nevada, far too close to people, plants and animals for that to be considered alright. The contamination is huge and so obvious to me, as I pass through and very reminiscent of the traces that I had picked up in the Great Victoria Desert in Australia. It was also wrong because though this town feigned a type of normality, letting people in and through the site, whilst calling itself a town, Los Alamos was hiding nuclear bombs in plain sight, at the heart of the community, where they hoped that no-one would notice them. They seem to be getting away with it.

The contrast between the good-hearted indigenous peoples, that I had seen in Santa Fe market square and the rather arrogant behaviour of this scientific community, just above it in the mountains, made me both angry and sad all at the same time. I knew also, as I passed through, that some good-hearted people had worked at this oxygen depleted mountain-top town, over the years, believing that what they did was in order to secure the future of peace-loving peoples the world over, against the evil tyrants that would happily destroy them. They may well have been doing the right thing at that time, back in the Cold War days, but it was hard to believe that the current situation was anything less than a charade and an attempt to manipulate for others' bad ends. I know, as I pass through, that even the government of this country are not really in control and that there is some other force at play, that will show itself here one day, or be revealed maybe, by some clever detective work of my own. Some revelations, some truths are coming and once revealed, it could get very ugly.

As I pass through the soil and the general terrain of New Mexico, I know that the ancestors of this land are deeply

79

concerned, they are grumbling and rumbling, which is never a good sign. They are not yet entirely awake enough to take back their power, but also they are not so very asleep that they are doing nothing about the situation, but rather, they are in a place somewhat like a somnambulist, slumbering, but unable to settle properly into sleep. They are looking for the truth too and the necessary pointers as they awaken, that will take them in the right direction, in order to take action. But they not yet ready to take the reigns and lead the way.

Being locked into the land has kept them here on earth, not yet released into the ether, where they might feel the freedom that I do. Their land-locked commitment to Earth and its people is commendable, but somewhat akin to a prison sentence, from which they can neither ascend nor escape. I feel deeply effected by the situation and these energetic grumblings which I know need to be understood. The freedom that I have had since I can remember, the freedom that has allowed me to explore with limited binding attachment has probably been my saving grace, my greatest strength.

Today, I feel a twinge of recognition of a weakness that I am developing on this journey of mine. This walk through time, space, geography, hearts and minds, is having its impact. How long do I continue in this vein before I lose that absolute freedom and find myself bound forever to this Earth and these peoples? Seeing the fate of ancient ancestors is a warning. I will keep a distance, I pledge, that will allow me to save myself, should it become necessary. I am torn. Whether to abide at an earthly level, or to raise myself up above it all, in a manner that will enable me to better see the truths of the world, to be closer to the light above, closer to the universal truth that awaits me and away from the petty day-to-day burden of earthly matters. I rest awhile and return to my Australian meditative state to ponder the situation and as I drift away these words, arriving on the warm, dry breeze, float through me............

.........*Dig deep, listen to your heart,*
Cast out fear and doubt and
allow the wind and elements to take you.
Let fire burn you, let water drown you,
Let thorns scratch you, let terrain graze and wound you.
Roll in the long, wet grass
and open yourself up to the elements,
Until you are inside out, upside down,
Both smaller and larger than you have ever been before.
Shine like the sun, twinkle like the stars and
Absorb like the blackest moment in history,
Time and space devour you and take you deep into the ALL
and spit you out like a nothing,
A nothing that cannot be destroyed, but spat out like a pip,

81

Ready to assimilate and nourish itself, ready to grow again,
grow afresh, grow anew.
A new YOU, a new dawn, re-invented and transformed.
Combining day and night,
good and bad,
happy and sad,
Large and small,
Fast and slow,
In and out,
Sane and insane,
Clever and stupid,
Arriving and leaving,
Hot and cold,
Oscillating to a point of perfection!
All brought together, wedded into one perfect
Being of Light and vibration at the highest level.
A vibration that could not have been reached any other way.
The vibration of the NOW,
The vibration of the Future,
A vibration that you can both sustain
and that will sustain YOU,
From now until the end of time………….

On leaving this place I am deeply moved and now feel
somewhat unsettled, but cannot pinpoint why. There is

trouble coming to planet Earth and I know that I have a part to play when it starts to kick off. Let's just hope, for the sake of all on Earth, that I am powerful enough, equipped and stable enough to make the right decisions. No small ask.

I fly South of here and find myself above a beautiful Mesoamerican pyramidal structure, that I know as I pass through, to have been built by the ancient Mayans. This is a sacred site that I am drawn into by the warmth and power of its internal energies. It has tales to tell of life before this jungle had been allowed to impinge on its sacred space and suck some of the power out of it, but it has some power yet and some secrets too, that will be revealed in the coming of the right time. There are many sites such as this one, all invisibly connected, that have similar significance. The megalithic structure at Sacsayhuaman in Peru is one, where huge multi-sided blocks have been created, no-one quite knows how, into one of the largest and most perfect jigsaw puzzles, made up of exactly crafted and perfectly fitting blocks of solid stone. I know as I pass through, that these stones were not carved by man. They were forged by a civilization, who long ago left the Earth, for the farthest reaches of the Universe, with every intention of returning one day to finish the job. What I cannot fathom, is why they left at all.

The beauty and mystery of these structures is a beguiling conundrum. As I linger, I allow my thoughts to drift off into the jungle, drawn initially by the sound of dripping water from within the canopy and then by the haunting sounds of the birds, monkeys and insects that dwell here. Such a contrast to the wildlife that I am familiar with in Sussex. It is relentless and I find myself in a trance, moving about the canopy, way above the tops of the vines and the trees, allowing myself to picture what life these sounds represent down below, without the need to see them at all. I lose hours this way and it becomes another welcome meditation after having felt the need to distance myself from the people of the Earth. This meditation helps the balance within to return and encouraged, I return to Europe.

Chapter 14: **Switzerland**

In all my days, thus far, exploring the beautiful
mountain villages and cities of Switzerland, not once have I
encountered one of those Cuckoo clocks that everyone bangs
on about.

What is it with people that they feel the need to culturally
stereotype nations? My observations of people the world
over, as I have passed through, is that they are largely all
the same. They are guided best and most truthfully by their
hearts and let down most badly by their minds.

Where the heart is listened to and the truth of its deepest
desire communicated to the rest of the person, so that the
obvious and simplest of actions can be taken, then generally,
the better is the end result. But once that identity kicks in
and starts running the show, then the hearts' battle is
largely lost. It strikes me that people can be their own worst
enemy, if they give their power away to others, or allow
themselves to be drawn into co-dependent or dominant and
submissive relationships. Nations do this all the time. What
I have noticed about Switzerland though, is that it rarely
gets involved in either of these modes of behaviour. It has
more often developed an aloof modus operandi, distancing

itself from others and developing an independent way of functioning in the world. A leader not a follower.

I do detect some arrogance in this and a righteous air of superiority, that few others could carry off, but the Swiss can, because they are actually very clever and it's somewhat justified. In their history with their particular choice of actions, they have saved themselves from being tarred with the same warring brush as most other nations and have not engaged in any international conflict since 1815. This land-locked nation has developed a clever survival strategy, since it cannot escape its five neighbours, that has proved most effective. They do say that necessity is the mother of invention, after all. So, It does not start fights; It does not get drawn into the fights of others; It remains neutral on the surface, whilst being quietly in control of the situation. The burning and unsettling question in my mind, as I pass through, is 'just what else is going on here, under this mask of seamless maturity and control, what are they hiding'?

Yet this place seems close to perfect with its temperate climate, where ski-ing in its mountains is some of the best in the world. Its southern most tip bathes in an almost mediterranean climate, where they make great wine.

Its 8 million people live in relative luxury, compared to most others on this planet and have taken absolute responsibility for the part that they need to play in reducing their carbon footprint and have fully embraced all renewable sources of energy that do not involve a sea.

They are fully independent of their neighbours, in that they neither share in the Union of Europe, nor the Euro and are admired hugely for their autonomy and great successes with money.

Their transparency around governmental matters and civil liberties has one of the best records in the world, the antithesis of their opacity and incredible discretion around money.

They are good with money, regardless of to whom it belongs and the whole world knows it and since this Earth seems to believe in money much more than any god or Mother Nature, this pretty much puts them in pole position. It is quite incredible to think that Switzerland was not once invaded during the two World Wars that ravaged Europe, but rather, afforded both sides a neutral space from which espionage was carried out and mediated communications imparted. It seemed to have had a somewhat charmed life through conflicts that destroyed so many other nations and whether that was their ability in diplomacy or whether other forces were at play, was something that had never been properly investigated. The lack of destruction in that early part of the 20th Century, certainly led to Switzerland having a head-start in getting on with building a brilliant modern economy and cultural structure that led the way across Europe.

The Swiss, not burdened by having to re-build themselves from the ground up, had maintained a higher vibration, that has allowed them to focus on developing the finer points of design, which they embodied in the Bauhaus School of Walter Gropius, changing attitudes the world over. The Latin name for the country, Confoederatio Helvetica inspired one of the most iconic typefaces ever designed, which encapsulated the very essence of what it meant to be Swiss, resulting in the Swiss School at Basel, spawning copy-cat design schools the world over.

These are good people, who have done good things. They created The Red Cross, which I know for sure has alleviated huge amounts of suffering across the whole Earth, when nations have warred and people have been the unwitting victims, caught up in the battles.

Sitting atop the Matterhorn, on the Italian side of Switzerland, I can see most of what is happening on the surface of this country, whilst also picking up on an odd and powerful vibration, an indication of what is happening below the surface too. There is an energy here that is familiar to me and I am being drawn to it, but find that I am intentionally resisting the call, out of caution and until I know exactly what I am up against.

Traveling towards Geneva, I come across the European Nuclear Research Facility, otherwise known as CERN, which strikes a familiar chord too, as I remember it was the desired destination of Pale Physics student over two years before. My vibration soars at the prospect that I might pass through and find him there, so that is just what I do, as I have never been much of a one for holding back and hanging with the tension of any given situation, but rather more quicksilver in my engagement with absolutely everything. It looks pretty high security, as I fly in from the mountains above. Reaching the facility, I can see scientists arriving back from lunch and others leaving for lunch, it's actually very amusing since those that are leaving mostly seem to have nothing but good coffee and food on their minds, almost rushing to get there after whatever type of morning they have had and those that are coming back seem to be feeling uncomfortable at having eaten or drunk just a bit too much. I can only think that they probably go through this same slightly painful routine every day, yet never learn.

There is a woman scientist arriving back after lunch and I can see that she has a very special kind of lightness to her. She almost glows all over, but particularly she is glowing in the head and shoulders area and she almost floats along on a cloud of calm. Conversely, there is a very unkempt male scientist, just leaving the building, who seems to be surrounded by a dark cloud of something very powerful indeed, certainly what I would describe as negative energy. I pass through to check him out and find that he has had a bad night. In fact it is one of a long line of bad nights that he just cannot shake off. The first was about a month ago, after a very exciting day when they had run a test of the Hadron Collider at CERN and unexpectedly, the feeling it had left him with had been bothering him ever since.

In his mind, I can see the scene of him returning home after that long day, to find a black cat on his doorstep, which must have been cold and hungry, because it dashed into his apartment as soon as the door opened. He noted that it was a very large black cat indeed, but decided to feed it and whoosh it out again as soon as he could. But he was a lonely scientist, with no friends, no partner or family that he could be bothered with, so he kept the cat for a few days, quite glad of the unusual company. It seemed to like him, which pleased him, so he kept on feeding it and telling it about his day at work. One night, when he was asleep in bed, he became aware of some movement on the top of the duvet and realised that it was the cat looking for warmth, so he went back to sleep, with a smile on his face. This carried on for a week and he just accepted that at last, something in the world was not repulsed by him, so he decided to let it continue. After almost three weeks, he had found that the cat seemed to be capable of dictating how he spent his evenings, not letting him read a book or play music. It would leap through the air and push things out of his hand. He started to feel quite scared of the cat, but didn't now know how to get rid of it. The night before I see him heading out for some lunch, was the night that had really put the cat amongst the pigeons.

The poor man had been awoken by the cat landing rather too heavily on the bed and in his annoyance, he had turned on the light, determined to chuck it out once and for all, never to return, but when he did just that and looked at the cat on the bed, he realised that it was not a cat at all, but a man. The man looked at him with sharp needle like teeth and a body covered in black fur, but not so dense that he couldn't see the skin underneath, though it did seem to cover his whole body. He could clearly see that the man had no tail and had he stood up on its hind legs, would have been about three feet tall. It had turned on him viciously at being discovered in the night and they had fought each other in the darkness.
The scientist was so terrified, that from somewhere deep inside him, and maybe a vague muscle-memory of practicing

Judo as a kid, he found the strength, not only to grab a hold of the beast, but to open the window of his bedroom and roughly chuck it out. He heard it land on the cobbled street and squeal loudly and then it had whimpered for some time, as it limped off down the street.

He had never experienced anything quite like that before and felt bemused and baffled and was far too terrified to sleep again at all after that, in case it found a way back into the apartment, so he sat up wrapped in a blanket with a cup of coffee, on a night vigil, just praying to a god that he had never allowed himself to believe in ever before.

I know that what he had experienced was actually real, as the residual memories of the events were still emblazoned on the visual part of his brain. He had seen it, it had happened, but he was now trying to come to terms with what it meant and whether or not he would ever really shake it off, or sleep again. Poor man. I leave him to search for something comforting to eat, knowing that we will meet again soon.

Just as well that I can pass through absolutely anything with ease, which of course I do.
The security guards are oblivious to my presence and even the very delicate energy indicators that seem to be mounted

everywhere, cannot detect such a very small thing as me, however powerfully charged I might have become in the past year or so. Especially when such a thing doesn't want to be detected.

I pass through numerous great minds as I wander about the facility and learn a good many things. I learn from an elderly Physicist, that the human mind isn't actually wired in a way to ever sufficiently comprehend the true physics of the Atom and that CERN's symbol representing the Atom and its structure, which has been their symbol for a long time, turns out to be a massively inaccurate oversimplification of an Atom's, which he knew from the start, when it was adopted and that is now currently understood by all. In fact they were the laughing stock of the learned world of scientists because of it for a while, which had caused him to endure some embarrassment in several social gatherings and conferences in scientific communities across the globe.   There are other things that trouble him a lot, to do with the direction of travel of the organisation. He also knows that a lot of things they are 'scientifically' investigating, don't stack up in the scientific community and he is concerned that his age is against him, with every likelihood that he will not know any or many of the answers that he has spent a lifetime seeking, before retirement and death come to him first. He seems vulnerable in his

93

dissatisfaction at the way things have turned out for him and there is resentment of the youngsters that have turned up in recent years. They seem to sail to the top and be given all the advantages and all of the current budgetary allocation to boot, whilst others have done all the legwork. This place is huge and seems to be an endless array of corridors leading to yet more corridors, which in turn open onto yet more corridors, with one special surprise when I find myself innocently entering something that purports to be a corridor, but that I instinctively recognise to be a path instead. I have never felt true awe such as this before. I am in awe of The Path that has opened out before me, a path that is so familiar to me, since it is a path for Atoms to walk. I walk The Path once, the whole 17kms and cannot believe how good it feels. I will be coming back here, I decide, as I travel this path of destiny, as soon as I have explored the rest of the facility and ascertained whether or not Pale Physics Student is here. My assumption is that I will pick up on his energy, as I pass through walls, doors and laboratories, but that proves unhelpful, as the place is just a buzz with so many new energies, that it is like looking for a needle in a haystack. I need to adopt a more logical and systematic approach. I remember, from passing through, that Pale Physics Student planned to be so exceptionally good, that he would be accepted onto the CERN Apprenticeship Program. So I head for Human Resources, to see if he is anywhere on their radar yet. HR is not hard to find, since it's an up-beat and positive hub of people, who are making connections between this facility and the rest of the world. Seeking out the very best people to support this huge scientific vision. I spend what seemed like hours, but was probably only a second or two, looking through the list of current employees, from which he is sadly absent. He is also absent from the Interns and Apprentices list, as well as the list of those that will be joining the program in the coming 6 months. The disappointment that I feel is tangible, but I don't give up just yet, as I hover over the shoulder of the boy opening the incoming mail, only to see that his application has just arrived for consideration. So he's not here yet, but maybe I can make sure that he is here soon! The prospect of Atomic nepotism thrills me and I feel a satisfying vibration rise in me. Power.

Without a second thought, I pass through the young man's mind and plant the seed that this particular application belongs in the 'Highly likely' pile, which is exactly where he puts it and it is marked 'exceptional'. Not daring to do much more than that, I can see, from the email address, that Pale Physics Student is now at Imperial College in London, probably studying for his Masters, which is where I decide to head, to plant a seed in his mind that he has little to worry about with regards his application. A mind at peace is far more likely to do well in its Masters finals.

Chapter 15: **Coming Home**

It must be Winter in the northern hemisphere, since the days are so short, pale and uninspiring. This is not the best time to be returning to England, I decide and cannot imagine how I had managed to get my timing so badly wrong. I remember The Path that I walked that Winter before I left and the lack of stimulation on it whilst its fair-weather dwellers huddled inside keeping warm and dry. The high point had been what the lurking Photographer had captured in her lens and the joy of watching Crow Man, whom I hoped was still walking The Path on my return. I needn't have worried as he was the very first soul that I encountered as I walked The Path for the first time in almost three years. I passed through him to see how he was feeling out here on The Path on such a chilly morning and was surprised to find that he was as snug as he could be, because his granddaughter had bought him a batch of 10 mini hot water-bottles for Christmas for moments such as this, all kitted out with little knitted jackets each with a heart on, which his wife had lovingly filled with boiling water from the kettle just minutes before his departure from home. He had one down each Wellington boot snuggling his ankles, one in each of his jacket pockets, where he could pop his hands when his gloves were not quite toasty enough.

Two had taken each of his back trouser pockets, to keep his bum cheeks warm and the last two were in the front pockets of his shirt. As he moved, the bottles waggled purposefully and the warm air wafted around filling all the gaps in between and there were many gaps in between, since his clothes were as ever, rather roomy. The crow food on the menu today was scraps from last nights fatty pork dinner and some old bread that he had dipped in dripping from last Sunday's roast beef. This was some of their favourite food, since it had some sustaining energy in it, which just plain bread could never deliver. After the harsh winters that they had endured in recent years, they were determined to build some fortitude in their constitutions in case the kindly feeding stopped. As I passed through the heads of a few of the gathered crows, I picked up on their attachment to the old man and their concern for themselves should he leave them. I passed through Crow Man too, to check out his general state of health, only to find that he had never felt fitter or more contented. This, I passed on to the nearest crow, who then cawed it out loudly to tell the others that all was well in their world.

Leaving them to their communing at the top of the meadow at the side of The Path, I cast one last look back at them and am not surprised to see that the space surrounding Crow Man's head and shoulders is illuminated by a golden light.

98

My interest is soon drawn to something that is glinting at
the edge of the woods and moving closer in and swooping
under a low-lying bough, I come up in front of a
photographers' lens and I hear her gasp as I pass up and
into the upper branches of a tree. She is looking for clues
and I get the sudden idea that maybe I am one of the clues
that she's been in pursuit of and now found. What a fabulous
thought, to now imagine that she can see me, though no-one
else ever has! I like being seen by her, since she seems to be
engaging with the energies of things that others are too
scared or dull-witted to acknowledge. What takes me
completely by surprise in the next minute is the arrival from
the industrial estate, of a line of three, men all and focused
on the end result of being the best, better than the rest back
at base and unstoppable as they jog, jog, jog, turn the corner
once, jog, jog, jog and turn the corner twice in perfect
formation, until they hit The Path and crunching in unison
on the grit, they keep up a pace that others cannot match.
This is a sight for any sore eyes that might be watching. I do
not know for sure how long these three have been back
together, working as a team and suspect that things are not
entirely as they were before, that would be impossible
considering the vulnerability that had been exposed on that
November night three years ago. But here they are, a team
once again and though the pace is markedly slower than
before, doing what they did and still do best, putting on a
99

show of strength for the rest of the world to see. I pass through each in turn to check out what's really going on here, starting with No.1 on the right, who is just pleased to have his mate back at work and still able to come out training with them. I pick up on his genuine concern that he doesn't want No.3 to overdo anything, but determined not to undermine his standing in these early months of returning to training, even though he'd returned to work some 12 months before. No.2 in the middle is struggling with the return of No.3 to the team, since he is convinced that he could have killed them all and that he has proved himself to be the weakest link and should be treated with extreme caution. Very different reactions from these two fellows. Returner, No.3, on the other hand is chuffed to bits that he's been welcomed back and that he is doing so very well. They have no idea how far he has come and how much this means to him and they cannot begin to really know what a gargantuan effort he is putting in just to keep up with this much slower pace. He is grateful for his life and he is grateful for the return to work. He is also grateful that the essence of the word 'team' has been preserved in their act of accepting his place back in it. I decide to keep all of their separate thoughts as just that. Separate. They each need to come to terms with their own individual insecurities for this team to have a future. Watching them go by, I travel to the start of The Path at the upper corner of the meadow, near the garage. There are some familiar faces to be seen, some walking dogs, others walking themselves. I know that Pale Physics Student won't be amongst them, since he is up in London focusing on being the best Physicist they have seen in a decade or so. My thoughts quite naturally turn to Moody Blonde, since the last time I saw her, they were together and so very much an item, but her vibrant energy is obviously absent too and I have to content myself with ascertaining her whereabouts after my imminent trip to seek him out. For the rest of the day, I content myself with the simple pleasure of exploring The Path from the top end, through its middle, to the bottom end and all the way back again. I must have traveled The Path at least a thousand times that day, familiarising myself with every detail, every shrew and mouse, every seed plotting its germination, assimilation and realisation come the warmer weather. I like the energy generated by these plotting seeds, so full of potential and so perfectly prepared for life. I am happy and more contented than I can remember being in a long while. In the afternoon I see some unexpected joggers, that I had only associated with Summer and fair weather, such as the young lad, who had felt himself such a fraud that first day that he'd trod The Path alone for the first time, but now much older and very confident in both his physical status and his right to roam and also very much more mature and accomplished than at 16. He was following Red-head and

101

would imminently be overtaking her, had he not slowed his pace just a little, in order to relish the beauty of her fluid stride for just a few seconds more. Cheeky young rascal, she's old enough to be his mother! Once alongside her, he picks his pace up a little and whizzes on by and off like a rocket towards the top end, blushing in the cool breeze, all the way.

Satisfied that all is well in this little outdoor corridor this morning, I leave it and head for London, to explore that which I might find on my way to Imperial College and to see what has come to pass in the life of Pale Physics Student and the Moody Blonde. Just to make it all a little more interesting, I decide to take the train, passing from carriage to carriage and passing through as many heads as possible, playing cupid here and there, as well as playing devils' advocate by passing thoughts from head to head and leaving people in some hilarious states of confusion. What struck me as being particularly interesting were the conversations that had sparked seemingly out of nowhere, shortly after I had passed through. By the time we drew into Victoria Station at 8:30am, that train was buzzing with excitement from end to end. Like a happy hive of bees, on wheels.

Victoria Station is incredibly exciting, with people crisscrossing the concourse in every direction. Some, coming in from the side street, still glistening from the sleet and rain that had landed on them out in the Winter street. Others coming out of the mouth of the tube station much drier, but surrounded by a type of steam that is only emitted from damp clothing that has been overheated in an enclosed space. The tumble-drier train.

Nobody looks very happy, just focused on being somewhere else and just wishing that there wasn't a journey still to be endured between now and wherever that place is. Incredibly, these people, though moving at speed, all manage to avoid smashing into each other, so there is absolutely no damage whatsoever. I am impressed. As they pass by the main entrances in and out, many of them are grabbing the Metro from the newspaper stands to catch up on what has happened since they left the city last night. The headline on the paper shows an image of a strange cloud, the first of its kind to be seen anywhere on Earth, that has appeared above Switzerland. Apparently the cloud was seen spinning in a perfect circle and not being carried far by any prevailing wind, maybe just a little off to the same side, but always centering itself back above the same spot again and again in just a matter of minutes. The cloud has apparently sat there for days on end, rumbling and glowing from within, as though it had its own internal storm fighting to get out. The headline reads: 'Clockwork Clouds Go Cuckoo over Alps!' No one from the Swiss Government is available to comment at the present time. Under that is a second article about the need for people to take personal responsibility for reducing carbon emissions, since the government is struggling, year on year, to meet their pledged 2020 carbon emissions reduction target and arguing that it either needs an extension of time or a reduction of target. Sounds like data manipulation to me.

I know, from passing through the Station Managers head that there are delays on the underground, so although it would have no effect on me since I can pass through anything, I don't need to dwell in the negative energies or the frustration of others that this will create, so I go over ground instead. I whoosh out of the exit down the side of M&S and straight out to the bus station at the front, up over the rooftops and off towards Green Park, heading for Exhibition Road in South Kensington, to find pale Physics Student, if he is there.

In the chilly winter air, London looks beautiful. There is still much frost lingering on the rooftops of the better insulated buildings and where the sunlight has yet to creep. Everything seems to be glistening as white turns to wet, which in turn evaporates into the sky, to create some more clouds that will float off, taking the moisture with them. There are remnants of dark sludgy snow at the edge of the pavements, where it has been piled up to make way for pedestrians and I am aware of the constant trickling sound of the melting snow as it runs down into the gutter. The dynamics of such a seemingly passive process are fascinating to me, this cycle of cold water falling as snow, the air's capacity to keep the snow for a while, in spite of a temperature rise and then the slow return to liquid that freely flows away, only to return again somewhere else, continuing the cycle until the weather changes with the seasons and Winter becomes Spring.

Imperial College is in sight as I zoom up from the bottom of the road, past the Natural History Museum on my left and the Victoria & Albert Museum on my right, the Goethe Institute on my right too and then the next stop, just before The Royal Albert Hall and the Royal College of Art at Kensington Gore, 'Imperial College' to the left, where the brains reside on this side of town. I have not been here before, so have no idea where to start looking for my favourite Physicist, so I take up a pole position in the lobby of the main building, as a sensible place to start my search and see whether I can pick up on his energies emanating from any part of the surrounding rooms. I have all day and figure that he, unlike me, will have to pass through this way at some point.

Clever people enter the building. I can tell, just by looking, that they are clever because they are bespectacled and have made a conscious decision not to expend any energy or thought whatsoever this morning, on what they are wearing. They remind me of the rather scruffy and troubled scientist that I saw at CERN a few days before. They all have either a rucksack or a briefcase full of very important books, papers and notes. The handwriting is indecipherable. I pass through a good many bags, intrigued to find out what they might contain. What do clever people need for an average day at University? Bananas are popular, as are tissues, both in and out of packets, both used and unused and antihistamine, lots and lots of antihistamine.

Everyone, without fail has a warm knitted hat and some gloves and are mostly all still wearing their scarves, draped loosely about their shoulders because that is the suave thing to do. This is as much of a fashion statement as you will ever get here, I decide. There are also quite a few asthma inhalers and cold and flu remedies of one sort or another, tucked into easily accessed side pockets and a much larger number of comic books, containing a huge array of Super-hero stories, than I find acceptable for intelligent adults!

Every student has either an i-pad or a laptop with them and some have both. I note that they are all wearing their glasses, since they need them at all times it seems. Diving into and passing through student bags proves to be quite a delightful distraction for a while, so much so that it takes my attention away from watching whose passing through the lobby, until I am drawn back to my task by hearing a familiar voice. It is Moody Blonde, calling out to someone, who is coming down the stairs and who naturally turns out to be Pale Physics Student. I am complete. It is obvious that they are both very happy to see each other and they fall into each other and into immediate and comfortable conversation. This is a relationship standing the test of time and I am rather pleased with myself. They are talking about his application to CERN's Apprenticeship scheme and the fact that he has just received an email asking him to attend an interview in a months time, with a view to him joining the next batch of masters graduates, if he passes muster. There is a need for some excellent preparation, as they have also invited him to prepare a proposal for the doctorate that he would like to undertake whilst working there. Which if accepted, they will fund. They are obviously of a mind to take on only the most capable and determined of academics, who will remain with them for at least 5 years. They are prepared to invest in him. He feels proud, wanted and on top of the world. She is also very proud of him and is now feeling that she has let herself down by avoiding her studies for so long and now finding herself about three years behind where she could have been. She laments that her parents are poor

107

and curses the government for bringing in punitive student fees that she cannot bear to burden herself with, but is also very pleased at having found herself a University in Germany that will take her next year to study a combined Psychotherapy and Neuroscience degree in English and for less than £1,000 a year. She will get there one day, in spite of her limited funds and she will be the very best that she can be, you wait and see.

Before I leave his side, I pass through the shiny bright mind of Pale Physics Student and the rogue in me decides to tell him a little of Venus and Mars, so that in his very core, he innately knows the truth of what is there and what visiting probes would find, which I feel him acknowledge with a "how do I know that so completely? Yes, I do know that to my very core, so now let me prove it", kind of a thought.

The very best of thoughts.

Chapter 16: **In Sussex**

A few months on and Moody Blonde is returning to Brighton this afternoon, after many weeks hanging out with her favourite physicist in London. She has had a lot of fun, whilst he has been deeply buried in his studies, wandering about the streets of London, visiting all of the museums and monuments that are largely free for everyone to explore. She has determined to make the best use of London while she has the chance. Her favourites are the V&A, largely for its huge span of artefacts from across the centuries and also the geological parts of the Science Museum complex. She has a fascination with rocks and crystals and all things that have been dug out of the ground and I have spent a lot of time alongside her, so that I could gauge her immediate responses to things. She has such an enquiring mind and an innocence that enables her to ask the unusual and the unexpected question. We had a lot of fun in the earthquake room, where she stood in the dark until everything shook so much that she fell over a few times, though it naturally had no effect on me. Bearing witness to the experiences of others, is as good as it gets for me. There was a capacious room, with exceptionally high ceilings, full of old oak display cases, containing every mineral and crystal known to man, that doesn't pose a risk to human health. Those are stored somewhere else. Many of these are familiar to me, since I have traveled the world, both on its surface and below ground as well, often deep-diving into the soil to see what lurks beneath. The caves that I have found, that man has yet to, that are full of the largest crystals you could imagine, would cause a global sensation should they be uncovered. There are caves along the crystal grid of the earth, that many consider to be a figment of someone's imagination, but I know to exist, that could easily be pinpointed and uncovered, with just a little planting of knowledge from me. But I know that the time of their revealing is not down to me as there are other powers in charge of that. That knowledge belongs in a much greater master plan that will be revealed in the fullness of time. It fills me with excitement though, to know that they are there, just biding their time and ready to shine in all their glory, come the day. My hope is that they will be sufficiently powerful, once revealed, to counter some of the really bad stuff that I can feel is coming. The 7 miles of corridor at the V&A proved to be a place of both comfort and joy to us. The architecture alone was enough to elevate the spirits and lift me to a higher place, well as high as the ceilings would allow, which is in reality to quite a height by local standards. I was drawn in and dragged down a little by the stained glass and wrought iron works that filled one room. They carried some pretty tortuous energies with them, filled with a gothic

darkness and residual fear that no-one should ever have
been close to. It never ceases to amaze me, the ability of
objects and structures to harbour the vibration of the events
that have happened in their vicinity. Some pretty fiery
sermons have been told within the confines of those stained
glass windows and some really nasty torture has been
carried out by some of that heavy metal.

I felt the continuing vibrations emanating from everything
in the gallery. Moody Blonde did not linger in that place for
long, since she was in search of enlightenment not echoes of
human suffering.

At the end of her London time, she leaves to return to
Sussex to make preparations for the move to Germany.
Determined to arrive there in good health and good spirits,
she takes to The Path every day without fail. Hitting The
Path first thing in the morning seems to work the best,
allowing her to spend the rest of the day planning, phoning,
sorting the final details around finance and accommodation
and improving her written and spoken German too of
course! She is grateful to her Physicist for being an excellent
German student himself as they often hold lengthy
conversations with each other, which has built her
confidence enormously. She is still pinching herself, unable
to believe her luck in meeting such an amazing young man,
who saw the world as she did and I know as I pass through,

that she is hoping to spend a good deal of her life with him, if he'll have her. I quickly whizz back to London to let him know that she feels this way about him and to make sure that he innately knows it to be true, since we all need a little certainty in our lives. Cast out doubt. In the early morning light, when Moody Blonde hits The Path, its as though every local creature is welcoming her with a cheery "hello". Indeed that is her perception and also the truth of the matter, which I learn as I pass through the sentient parts of each of them. Even the Chalk-hill Blue butterfly is pleased to see her beauty and grace, which it equates with its own. There is a resonant recognition that is reflected between them. There is a blaze of glorious poppies in red, pink, dusty purple, white and an almost black, all populating the small bank between The Path and the road. Their fragility is unmatched as it sways in the early morning sun, which even before breakfast is already comfortably warm. The sky opens out before her as she runs, with its cerulean blue tint and a few faint cirrus clouds, harbouring icy crystals that will be gone in but a few minutes more.

There are skylarks up high, singing at the top of their little lungs, telling the world that they are glad to be alive. A woman walks a French bulldog, who looks a little reluctant and I know, as I pass through that it's hoping to be picked up. It's giving her sad eyes, but chuckling to itself because it always works as a strategy and the poor devoted woman ends up additionally exercised, indeed much more so than the animal. I pass through the dog's mind and tell it that she'll never fall for it again, then take the truth of what the dog has always been thinking back to her and for the first time in over 2 years, the nonsense stops and balance is restored. Today I am a pragmatic Atom.

Moody Blonde runs The Path, remembering that fateful day when she and he had inexplicably collided and runs through their subsequent joyful conversation, when he had apparently made playful reference to them being like colliding atoms in the Hadron Collider.
She'd not heard of it before that day, so was quite thrilled to think that he had so swiftly made a link from her to his beloved physics. Moody Blonde had got used to seeing the regulars on The Path. I was there with her always, though she never knew it. One of her favourites and mine is Crow Man, whose connection to nature fills me with hope for us all. He has truly showed the way with his compassion for the crows and his boundless enthusiasm for life.

This morning shocked us all, when instead of walking or cycling, he came whizzing up the lower side of the meadow, visible from The Path, on a Lambretta. He had on an ancient helmet, that I suspect he had been wearing since the late 1950s. His wild white hair flowed out the sides and at the back as he flew along towards nobody knew where. Maybe he wasn't headed anywhere in particular, just enjoying the air and the freedom and giving his bike a bit of a run to celebrate the arrival of the better weather. As ever, he was a sight for sore eyes and everyone who saw him felt their hearts lift. Such a blithe spirit and a credit to the human race.

The whole day was light and airy. Even the golfers did a better job of things, managing to keep their balls on the right side of the road, on the greens today. There were days when it didn't matter whether you were on the other side of the road, you still had to duck to avoid the wayward shots. The conservation group had found in excess of 50 balls in one short season of clearing rubbish from the woods at the side of The Path and people were endlessly finding them in their gardens or hearing them crack roof tiles. A small pocket-money fortune could be made in reselling them back to the golfers, if only some enterprising teenager could be bothered to collect them all up. As I follow Moody Blonde this morning, I count 17 Magpies on the meadow at the side of The Path. If 7's for a secret never to be told, then 2x7 made 2 secrets and the other 3 are most definitely for a girl. Perhaps Moody Blonde had 2 secrets that had to be kept, I thought. But oddly for me, I didn't pass through to find out what they might be. I had shown discretion for probably the first time, maybe because I was so fond of her and knew that I would find out anyway soon enough. Sometimes it's just good to have something to look forward to and a secret is a secret after all.

The Magpies were being very argumentative and flying up and down from grass to tree-top and then back again. They were chasing each other, as if there were some kind of hierarchy that I could not fathom. It could have been play, but seemed rather more boisterous than normal. It was when I came closer that I could see that a Magpie from their group had been hit by a golf ball flying across the green and over the busy road at the side of that path, knocking it into the gutter and they all seemed to be very concerned indeed.

There were 5 of them, that flew down to where their fellow lay and who were nudging at it gently, each in turn, with their beaks. One flew off, coming quickly back with some dry grass, which it lay on the now dead bird, then the next did the same and the next, until they had all paid their respects to the fallen bird with focused solemnity. I learn, from passing through, that this was the male mate of one of the females in the group and that though they might only live for 5 years, that they had paired 4 years previously and had mated every year since then, so for her this was indeed a sad passing and to see them pay such respect with her for their fellow, was heartening to witness. As the sun became hotter still, all of the slugs that seemed to linger unnaturally long on The Path this morning, were attempting to escape from drying up, heading for the still moist grass to preserve their lives for yet another day. They seemed to know that few birds would touch them, because of their bitter taste and the awful stickiness that they created in the beak, indeed so powerful that it might clam it shut. There was a frog lingering though, which was rather more of a worry for them, since they had a liking for them in spite of this. This life and death cycle was unfurling all around me, everywhere I roamed. Everything linked to death by some acute point along its lifecycle, either at the beginning, middle or end of life. Nothing was ever wasted, it seemed, since even the uneaten dead would rot or turn to dust and eventually their nutrients would be subsumed into the burgeoning life opportunity of something just starting out. Nature is an opportunist and never ungrateful for whatever comes its way. Looking back at the touching scene with the Magpies and considering their violent and vandalistic reputation, its easy enough to paint them as aggressors, who would gladly pick at the sores on the back of a horse or a cow and would dive down to grab carrion smudged on the road, or fly off with the eggs of smaller birds, but to have witnessed their tender respect made me accept that their

116

behaviour was not without thought or consideration, since they had not devoured or even pecked once at their fellow fallen bird. Impressive.

Chapter 17: **Commuting**

The distance between Brighton and Geneva is 638 miles and one hour difference in time. For the average euro-commuter, that can be problematic since flights leaving the UK early in the morning will rarely get you to your destination before lunch. For me there are no such problems since I can be there in a nanosecond, or the blink of an atomic eye, should I so choose. Something that I have become very good at is travel, whether it is simply from the beginning of The Path to the other end of it, or up, up and away to distant planets, they are all the same to me. I quite like the linear nature of this type of travel, since it gives me the opportunity to process whatever has been happening around and about. I cannot call it 'time to think', since I cannot know that I do much of that, but I certainly process a lot and I can react. I am sparked off by the energy of things or in things, which sets off a reaction in my little atomic body, which I might choose to describe here in terms that you will understand. I am also triggered by the thoughts that I find in people's heads as I pass through, again in an energetic way. Sometimes I cannot see how I am likely to react until it just...happens! A bit of a hot-head, some might say. I have tried commuting in a wide range of styles. Taking the Eurostar part of the way and then whizzing on out through the glass of the window and across country to get to my destination, which these days is CERN.

At other times I have taken a boat and then a train across numerous countries to get there, or 'en avion', which is great fun too. As you must know by now, I don't actually need any of these modes of transport to get me anywhere, but I choose to mimic what humans do, because I enjoy their company and the thoughts that I gather from their heads, as I pass through. I have learned a huge amount communing and commuting with human beings. I have learned very little passing through the minds of the average rodent or bird. You humans harbour a huge amount of interesting knowledge and conversely, some rather rodent-like thoughts too when you are tired, hungry or cold. Sometimes when I decide to commute, I pretend to be with someone, maybe taking the role of their imagined husband or wife, or a work colleague with whom they are having an in-depth conversation. A few times I have pretended to be someone's badly behaved child, just for the sheer hell of screaming and shouting at the top of my imagined voice and to let the powerful vibrations shock their way through those around me in a carriage. For the life of them, they cannot work out why they suddenly feel so uncomfortable, in the relative normal calm of the carriage, but maybe it brings back a bad memory of previous suffering at the hands of their own offspring. I will take the time to understand this behaviour of mine one day, when I am in the mood for some self-analysis and reflection, but all I know at the moment is that it gives me a sense of power and private satisfaction. Cause and effect really keep me engaged. I speculate that Moody Blonde might consider me to have a personality disorder, once she starts her studies in Psychotherapy and Neuroscience, if she were ever unlucky enough to meet me as one of her patients. Pale Physics Student has moved to CERN, he's been there since the end of August. His new role secured as a very lowly Apprentice, yet with 2 first class degrees in his portfolio and working towards his doctorate exploring the 'Atomic response to outside influence'. This PhD even, will not be enough to satisfy the scholarly and somewhat snobbish world of science, as he will also be expected to complete a post-doctoral thesis after that, if he expects anyone in the world of research to take him even vaguely seriously. He intends to be taken seriously, so they had better watch out as I know how determined he is to give them all a run for their money. Almost as determined as I am to help him. The reason for his fortnightly commuting, at the moment, is because his hearts desire still lives in Sussex and will continue to, until she moves to Germany at the end of September. Her University term begins the second week of October and she is earning and saving as much money as is humanly possible, whilst still keeping

120

every other weekend free to keep the flame of love alight. Once she arrives at Freiberg, to study Klinische Psychologie, Neuro-und Rehabilitationswissenschaften, they both know how important it will be for her to focus. They will both focus then, knowing that they are only just over the border from each other pursuing their dreams and giving each the unconditional support that they need, to cope with the inevitable demands of their new lives.

I take it upon myself to become the unseen go-between, firstly between CERN and Sussex and later, crossing the border at least 4 times a day, to keep their connection and thoughts of each other accurate, alive and well. I wonder sometimes whether any of this love between them would ever have happened, had it not been for my reckless intervention on The Path almost four years ago. Yet I do not feel guilty for having manipulated the situation, after all, isn't that what life is anyway, a set of chance events and encounters that can lead somewhere or nowhere, depending on what path you choose to take at each of these pivotal moments. I might have been the cause of the encounter, but I pretty much left them to it once the initial introduction had been made. I doubt that, had I made my hero bump into Froufrou, that they would have made it beyond a first date, or even to a first date, though I suspect that I might have made him want to give up jogging that particular path once she thought she had a possible date to look out for each day. They had nothing in common, which I knew as soon as I passed through. I could even have unwittingly ruined his whole life since then and he might never have made it to CERN. Such power, it strikes me, needs careful handling or it could become like a drug, which could be misused. Each day, I decide that I should take the most positive thought that she has about him and the most positive thought that he has about her and plant them firmly in the others' mind, so that all or any doubt caused by separation is cast out. If only people realised that they needed to do this for their nearest and dearest, they could nurture such powerfully positive and lasting relationships. I guess that people born into balanced families and nurtured to a state of absolute self-confidence, would never struggle with any of this, since they would always be certain about their own importance in the world. But sadly humans are seemingly all fed doubt for breakfast, lunch and supper it seems to me, which is the cause of so much misery. I see it as my job to nurture this pair, in the way that the perfect godparent might do, to help my charges fare as well as possible as they make their way in the world. The realisation that I am oscillating between helpful and petulant, good and on the verge of evil, is dawning on me. My vibration must have fallen lower than when I had spent time meditating and walking the Shaman path in Australia, so I resolve to raise it up again, so that whatever I do in this world has the most positive effect. The higher my vibration, the closer I will be to enlightenment. Enlightenment, both mine and that of others, is after all my overarching aim.

(End) The End is a very final place for any or all to arrive at.

Chapter 18: **Playing dirty with the Scientists**

Everyone takes science so seriously, I have noticed this over the many years since the matter created at the dawn of time turned from soup into people. Maybe trying to make sense of it all? Like a small fish being eaten by a bigger fish and then eaten by yet a bigger fish still, this ever-escalating hierarchy of the un-scientific judgement of others, being meted out across the whole scientific community. No achievement is ever quite enough it seems, like a pushy parent who would rather have a feverish and near suicidal striver on their hands, than a happy failure. So, if you have a GCSE in maths or biology, it should at least have been taken early, or very quickly have become an 'A Level' achieved first time and if you have one of those, you should have at least all three sciences covered and in addition, they should all be A*s in order to be considered worthy of entry to the finest Universities. Then at University, only a first will do, followed, of course, by the obvious Masters level completed in double-quick time, with no light or breath in between and no time to sneeze and there will be no top job appointments for anyone without a PhD at least. Then even the best graduates will not be taken at all seriously in the world of scientific research without a post doctoral thesis in something really ground breaking and thus it continues in a very bitchy and back-biting fashion ad-infinitum. It is reminiscent of divide and rule and has a whiff of the corrupting influence that knowledge and power brings. None of this can be healthy, nor, surely the reason why people were put upon this benevolent, bountiful and beautiful Earth?

I have watched many young people struggle and suffer and fall by the wayside, terrified to take a gap-year, or to try something out that was a little off-beam, but could potentially have really captured their heart or their imagination. I also know, that the very best scientific discoveries have been uncovered by the dreamers, who have allowed themselves the freedom to think outside the box, to drift a little. Those that kept their noses to the establishment grindstone, very rarely did anything much more than the dogs body work of another colleague, more senior or influential than themselves. No Genius.

So, here I find myself, the least qualified in Earthly terms, but older, wiser and better informed than any of these

Scientists that currently surround me, diving in and out of
their heads in the hope that I might learn something new.
Every fact that their craniums house, is yesterday's news to
me, since I was there when most of these events happened,
about which they are endlessly theorising. The saddest part
is that they have got most of it wildly wrong because they
are coming at everything with such closed minds. The
temptation to set them straight is huge, but I am saving
enlightenment for a certain favoured Physics student who is
coming their way. This game of forwarding his career, that I
plan to play, will keep me mightily busy and entertained for
many years to come, since I know how resistant this group
are in their acceptance of anything new. I also know that
they could come face to face with an alien spaceship on a
Monday morning, yet publicly deny its very possibility,
meanwhile back at base they are planning to send yet more
spaceships of their own making up to ever more farther
flung planets than before in the hope of finding alien life. If
a ship arrived without proper warning, or if it arrived and
then swiftly disappeared again, then they would probably
conclude that it had never really happened. So in response
to their endless nonsense, I will play a game with these
scientists, a game of test tubes, undeniable facts and proof,
all delivered through my brilliant and jolly physics prodigy.
Even he will be wondering how such undeniable truths and
facts are channeling through him, but he will go with the
126

flow as I quiet his mind and give him the benefit of my wisdom. I will plant the outrageous and the unacceptable and when they all go wildly into reaction, I will pull the absolute proof out of their own research, so that they can doubt him no more. My magical job will be to weave the threads of all relevant theories in with a whole lot of new and innovative thinking on behalf of the child genius at my side. They will hate him for it and they will try to bring him down, but I will make it my unwavering job to make sure that it all hangs together, so that he doesn't end up hanging........at all.

Having commuted hither and thither, to see his girlfriend for the first few months at weekends, my physicist is well liked and not seen as the competitive and hungry aggressor that some other recently arrived graduates have shown themselves to be. They who'd arrived and were so desperate to make their mark, that they had not yet dared to leave again. He has been labeled as benign by most of the scientists who have met him and also by his fellow graduates, but his substantial talents have been noted. No threat.
Maybe a bright one to utilise, for their own ambitions. This is great news since it allows him to move freely, without suspicion and gently embed himself, feeling very much at home and comfortable in this rather competitive

environment. He is not at all anxious since I have daily equipped him with messages of comfort about his love life and about his considerable abilities as a scientist. There is no self-doubt, which is exactly where I need him to be. I feel no guilt whatsoever about this state of affairs, since I know exactly what others know and in many cases how very lucky they are not to have been found out yet, for how little that can sometimes be.

Pale Physics Student, which will remain his name until his PhD is completed, is now more prescient in his daily activities, having agreed with Moody Blonde, that they will not be getting in each others way when focus is required, which it now is. His first objective is to find out what all of the major projects are at this research establishment. What he realises soon enough is that there are things that people speak freely about; things to which people allude; and things that cause people's eyes to flicker and twitch uncertainly, as if someone might be watching or listening in. The nervousness is palpable, so I pass through the minds of these scientists first, since these are the projects that I need to focus on for now.

There is one particular lab-coated individual, who cannot have cleaned his teeth in years, since they are coated in so much yellow that it's falling into his mouth as he speaks.

128

This is a nervous man whom I have seen before, whom I know has a brilliant mind, but has been locked in the lab for so long that he has no friends or family that he can remember. His parents do wonder whether they will ever see him again, but he thinks of them rarely. What he is thinking about, every minute of every day and every night, is the machine that he is building, that will create weather, the kind of weather that could make or break a whole country. It's famine or feast time once this man's job is done, wherever he uses it. The project has unhinged him hugely as he is not really emotionally equipped to play God. Recent events in his apartment have also caused him huge anxiety and I know from our previous encounter, that he is scared of his own shadow these days. He has a dark energy close to him that is not of his making, nor is it a part of him, but it is strong and lingering. I know, from passing through this brilliant mind, that his machine can be used anywhere and that it is so small that it can be brought in on a camping trailer and set up without access to power, just a little solar encouragement. It just needs to be placed somewhere where nobody will tamper with it and left to create its own local climate changes. You set it to drought and that is what will be created in less than a month. Set it to flood and that can be achieved in less than a week. Tornadoes can be whipped up in less than an hour and sent off in a direction of your choosing.

129

What amazes me, when I pass through is that there are no thoughts in his mind to create the perfect ambient temperate climate in which all species can thrive, as though he has by-passed happy and normal and can only deal in the worst extremes. So I decide to scramble his thoughts by making him think of nothing but the absolute importance of cleaning his teeth, since I can see that to all who surround him that this is the immediate problem to be tackled. It takes less than an hour for him to leave the building in search of a chemist shop where he can purchase paste and a brush and to find a men's room where he scrubs at his mouth for the rest of the afternoon. There is blood, inevitably.

Once that little obsession has run its course, I will set him to obsess about the rest of his personal hygiene and then follow up with setting his thinking straight around his obligation to the planet and those who have every right to live happily upon it.

There is one quite elegant female scientist who gets my attention too, partly because she stands out as being in command of her world, based on outward appearance, but I know from passing through, that she is super-excited about whatever it is that she is working on. She has had a recent breakthrough, that she believes will make her name and allow her to lead much more prestigious projects in her future career. What she has yet to fathom, is that if she sees this project through to its inevitable conclusion, that there will be no future in which to run any projects of any sort at all. She has been tracking and uncovering the energetic streams and power links that run across the globe and that link the crystal grid buried deep enough in the earth, that the nodes of it are rarely uncovered. They are also rarely uncovered because there are guardians who have been keeping these secret for millennia and they are not very happy with what she has been up to.

They know that her project represents a real threat to the energetic balance of the whole planet and ultimately that this will effect the wider universe, so they would do almost anything to prevent her from using such sacred geology for some tin-pot scientific experiment. They will stop her.

For such a bright individual, she is showing incredible naiveté and an incredible lack of respect for things much older than herself and certainly much more important to the wellbeing of all. I put it down to the amount of time it has taken all scientists such as she is, to get this far and the undue pressure that they have been burdened with whilst trying to prove themselves in this critical community. She is at the top of her game and yet, when I pass through, all I can pick up on is the prevalence of fear of doing something that she fundamentally knows to be wrong, mixed with an absolute fear of failure. What a waste of brilliance that could otherwise be used to make life on Earth better for everyone. With her, I muse, there is an opportunity for her to be in receipt of some additional knowledge around what these guardians will do to her should she cross certain clearly defined lines. She also needs to feel some shame for the destructive intent that she has been nurturing.

There is a third scientist that I meet in the corridor, that I know from passing through his mind, is involved in the best known of the projects at CERN, he is working on splitting the Atom and trying to recreate the effect of the Big Bang, under controlled conditions. Who is he trying to kid? This kind of crazy is stupidity to such a degree that I am thrown by the prospect that he imagines that he would be in a position to analyse any of his data, post the 'controlled' Atom-splitting event. Nobody could begin to imagine what that might result in making happen, since the first time around it was a pretty random outcome that took millions of years to unfold, revealing what we have today on Earth and across the Universe. Nobody knows what might come out the other end this time, but I do know one thing for sure, what IS now, will be NO MORE.

He is troubled by the adverse publicity that his work is attracting. I know from passing through, that he has created an Electron Cloud effect, above the Large Hadron Collider machine, which runs in a tubular circle around the CERN facility. When the particle accelerator is whizzing around this huge underground circle, that circumnavigates nine villages underground, a huge cloud is created above ground, a cloud that is illuminated from within by the electrical discharge that it is creating within its interior atmosphere. It was the first appearance of this cloud that set our rather nervous scientist off on his path to develop his heinous weather machine.

The cloud above the Collider has been filmed and it has caused a hushed sensation in the area and on the internet. It seems that he is annoyed at the lack of privacy for his scientific works and is also determined to find a way to stop the cloud, so that the work can continue undisturbed. The last thing they need is to upset their tolerant Swiss hosts, since this project would not work anywhere else on the planet.

This Hadron Collider is the largest and most powerful of the particle colliders created by man. It is also the largest single machine in the world. This is a collaboration of over 10,000 scientists and engineers from over 100 countries, so is not such a secret project in reality, but there do seem to be some hush hush elements that are best left in the deepest

133

shadows. Its main role is to allow physicists to test the predictions of different particle physics theories and in particular to test the theories about the illusive Higgs Boson...I have walked this impressive path.

Chapter 19: **I am not alone**

Since the dawn of time, I have been wrapped up in my own little World, roaming about, criss-crossing the Universe, enjoying this amazing Solar system and appreciating being able to see everything that has unfolded around me. I felt the heat and the rushing speed of the Big Bang as the Universe whizzed out from a single point in an attempt to fill up all that Space. I was on it and in it from the very beginning, forged in the hottest heat at the dawn of time and impervious to subsequent danger. Autonomous and powerful, I am the Atom.

For thousands of years I actually believed that I was unique, that there was no other Atom quite like me, which logically is quite unlikely indeed! Why would that huge explosion have created only one of me? If something gets split, surely there will be at least 2 created? I did eventually realise that there must be more, but If I am indeed just one of many, I have puzzled ever since then as to why I have not yet met my twin, a sibling, or at least a distant cousin. I met the occasional similar thing, but nothing ever quite matched up, energetically speaking. I stopped looking for them after a while and just focused on the pleasure of watching the Universe unfold and the beginnings of emergent life. I fell in love with Venus and dwelled there a while and then I fell in love with Earth and all its abundant and diverse flora and fauna, where I spent millennia in an absolute state of bliss. These things diverted me from continuing to seek out things like me, until now. The moment I arrived at CERN, I could tell that this was a very significant development for me. The energy felt different. There was something about the place that made me feel at home, but oddly for almost a month after I arrived it was not obvious to me what was to reveal itself, until today when they started up the equipment. It hadn't run at all in months, It didn't run all the time as there were major preparations to be undertaken and technical repairs to be completed since the last time any piece of the equipment had been used.

Some of this stuff would have been years in its preparatory phase and only minutes in actual running time and then maybe, once those initial tests had been successfully completed the machines might then run for years at a time. Unless they broke down. Breakdowns being so costly meant that preparations were meticulous, in order not to make an error that might smash the budget and lose precious time on the project. If you consider that some projects were decades in their inception, planning and realisation, for some scientists that might span their whole career. No second chances it would seem for them, although I know and so should they, as good physicists, that they will of course come back around in some other energetic form. But plankton rarely get inside a lab as the lead on a project and are much more likely to end up in the Petri-dish. Not an attractive option for any scientist who would rather be the one playing God.

The potential to be removed from a project before it came to fruition was very much a reality for many, but too demoralising for most scientists to bear. As we know, they are under pressure to be the best; to perform; to win; to make new discoveries and failure on the type of projects that they see at CERN is simply not an option. As ever, I digress.

When they started up the machines, things changed. Suddenly there was 'more' in the air of the place. It started in the corridors, like the scenes you get at the gates of a venue, when a huge sporting event is about to happen, like an Olympics event or a football match. People start to gather, there are perceptibly more people in the street, on the pavements, filling the trains, all moving towards the venue. This is what started to happen at CERN, the corridors were full of scientists, all aware that 'it ' was about to start, so they had to get to their posts, wherever those might be. Maybe at a desk, or a computer, or getting ready to push a button; observe; take photos; pull out a plug; add some chemical into the mix; or more power into the machine. They were buzzing with anticipation and excitement and what happened next, I didn't see coming and I had certainly never experienced before.

Other stuff gathered too, energetic stuff that felt just like the energetic stuff that I had only ever associated with myself. That sounds rather egocentric, I know, but even if this sort of thing had always been happening around me in the past, it was the first time ever that I had been switched on to perceiving it all as it appeared.

I felt it coming. There was a vibration in the air of the corridor so subtle that I must have been the only one aware of it, though maybe there were sensors in equipment here that were picking it up too, I could almost hear the jabbering and laughing of the photons, molecules and atoms as they came into being in their millions and before I had time to work out what was going on I was surrounded, completely and utterly surrounded! If I'd had eyes, I would have wept for joy, but in the absence of eyes, I just started to vibrate which was a sure sign that I was getting excited. Being surrounded by the invisible, but being able to see it for the first time.

There were so many different sorts, that it was almost impossible for me to know what they were. I had heard about some of these, from passing through the minds of scientists across the centuries and now, here they were all around me. They were bumping into me and moving on to bump into something else and as we bumped into each other, all of us were getting faster and hotter as the machine picked up speed and started to do what it was designed to do, accelerate.

The scene showed a cacophony of coloured, energy-filled balls and light-beings, all dancing and bouncing about. It was like a celebration of atomic life, where collision was the friendly norm. There were moments when two touched and that caused their colour to change, or their light to fade, what happened to each seemed to depend on what they were made of and what effect the essence of one was having on the essence of another. Some were diminished by collision and others grew in stature. Some were even completely obliterated, since they seemed to be of a weaker constitution and when they were destroyed, their material 'being' either joined another or scattered to join the many, so none was ever truly destroyed at all, just changed or transformed. I was finding the whole experience very rewarding, since every time I collided with another weaker than myself, very often they ended up becoming a part of me and every time

139

that happened I became ever more aware that I was indeed one of a kind, growing in stature and strength. My ability to combine with others unlike me was very unscientific and should not have been possible, but it was possible because I was not like any other atom that I met here today and I guess had never been like any atom that I had unwittingly met in the past. As I was surrounded and submersed in the euphoria of the moment, something passed through US as a group, now that felt weird, as it literally cut a swathe through the energetic body of atoms and molecules that filled the corridor. We had become so connected with each other, that it was almost painful. I felt concern for the zillions of times that I had done that to you, beings and objects of the Universe and vowed that I would try to cut down on targeting any one individual too much, in case it caused a problem for them, either then or in their future. What I then realised was that what had passed through had indeed been you, my favourite physicist and I felt some satisfaction that you might have shared in some of the energy of my current joy. I decided to extricate myself from the mass and follow you as best I could along the corridor to wherever you were heading.

It caused me physical pain to pull myself away and I felt like a reveller being dragged from the party too soon, a little drunk and heady and also rather startled by my return to reality. It was obvious once I started moving again that although they seemed to disappear, that these new relations that I had discovered were in reality still there, but they seemed to fade into the background a bit, because I had disconnected myself from them, so I could move more freely and not feel the constant bashing into them. My focus now, was on Pale Physics student and I was eager to find out what he was up to.

He was moving at speed and so I decided that in spite of the potential risk, that I would pass on through, to see what he was thinking. I was thrilled to find that he was headed for the cause of all this energetic kerfuffle, which was being generated by the Hadron Collider itself, warming up. It had not been fully in use since 2013 and here and now, it was back in use for a second time, the second time since April. The plan back then had been to run it for 3 months, which they did quite successfully and then made the necessary adjustments to enable it to run for the following three years. In that 3 months, they had played 'merry hell' with the worlds press, local population and conspiracy theorists on the web, over the unexplained cloud that had appeared and grown and then lingered day and night, glowing and growing and creating its own interior light and lightning show, that was extremely threatening, hanging there above the nine villages that surround CERN. I follow my hero into
141

the main room, where the largest machine ever created on Earth, lives. It is huge and I am truly in awe. Man is very inventive indeed and this demonstrates some real skill. This circular corridor is where atoms and neutrons and other particles will walk and they will walk very fast indeed. It immediately reminds me of what I consider to be my home, on The Path in Sussex, where I have engaged with local people and the real world of weather and nature in the most fulfilling way. On The Path there, I had met the favourite characters in my world; Crow man, Red-head and Froufrou, Moody Blonde and Pale Physics Student and many more besides, they feel like family to me now, but here in the Hadron Collider I know that I will meet my real family, should I wish to. I'd met some of them gathering excitedly outside in the corridor just now and I loved that experience on so many levels, but whether I want to become a part of someone's wild and powerful experiment, I am not entirely sure. Especially this flawed man.

My Hero is speaking with the physicist that I observed briefly earlier and being told what his role in this will be today and that "if he doesn't fuck it up", that there will be other juicy tidbits for him tomorrow and potentially for the next 3 years. I know that he is thrilled to be in this room and on this project as it is obviously the one that he would have chosen, but it IS he, of all the new Apprentices, who has been chosen for the job and that is a massive acknowledgement of his obvious abilities. I feel huge animosity toward the scientist for his language, vague threats, arrogance, in fact a whole list of other things that I cannot quite identify, but also I feel so very proud of HIM, my boy, and decide to let him get on with things in his own style, but make a promise to us both, to keep a watchful eye on absolutely everything until his work is done for today and every day, until I am sure that he is safe and seen for the brilliant scientist that he is. I will be his guardian angel, because frankly in a place like this everyone needs one of those!

Chapter 20: **Atom Smasher**

Pale Physics student works in this room, with this team, for a whole month, before he is given any real responsibility. He shadows each member of the team, learning their jobs and getting to grips with the technology and the underpinning science. What I love about the situation, is that I can pass through the head of any individual that he is shadowing and regardless of their capacity for communications, which is largely near to zero, he 'gets it' every time, in an instant. They are not used to being understood so clearly, or so quickly and they like this young scientist very much for it, since it gives them a real sense of accomplishment at communicating successfully first time and often for many, for the first time in their lives. They love him, he becomes the easy one to deal with and so they always include him in discussions and meetings, since he becomes somewhat of a translator for them all in discussions with the wider team. They always ask for the 'new boy' to be included or invited and every time, he proves to be invaluable and by the end of the month, he knows more about this particular project than any one other individual on Earth. He 'is' the current Expert.

The lead scientist on the project is unsettled and not entirely sure now whether it was such a good idea to bring this chap in. He cannot deny his usefulness, since he does do exactly everything that he should and certainly is completely on the money every time. In fact he is almost one step ahead of everyone on occasion and always right, which is causing trouble since people are starting to ask his opinion and listening to him more than many of his seniors, so to prevent the trouble escalating, I decide to back off for a while, to let him appear a little less than super-human, just for a week or two, until things settle down again. I have also become aware that it has been disconcerting for him too, since he's never been this brilliant before and though he loves it, he is also concerned that he has become extremely visible. Sometimes it's best to be unseen, until you are truly ready to reveal yourself.

The truth is though, that he doesn't really need me now, since he has not only already got all of the necessary knowledge, but he's actually very good at retaining it and assimilating this information and coming to his own conclusions. He doesn't need me to think for him, he just needed me to tease the information out of those extremely tightly closed minds, he needed the raw materials with which he can now get to work.

I am a little concerned that the lead scientist on the project has a bit of an issue with my boy, so I decide to pass through to get a better understanding about what, other than science, motivates him. I am hoping that he will prove to be a thoroughly nice chap, that I don't have to worry about at all, but you never can tell. As I pass through, he is standing with a clip-board at the side of this huge machine, and very surprisingly, I find that he is actually in awe of its size and power. I find this amazing considering that he has been a part of this project for a decade and should have become used to the reality of it by now, I decide. What I find even more surprising and very alarming, is what thoughts are actually going through his mind at that point...firstly, although he is the lead scientist, with the best clip-board and full responsibility for a huge budget and the largest and potentially most destructive machine ever built, he is imagining himself dressed as a Super-hero, in a white and gold costume, with a flowing cape and golden ankle high boots, with Eros-like wings coming out of his heels and flowing golden hair, like some Viking invader. But what is worse, so much worse than that, is seeing that he has a capital 'A' on his chest and he calls himself 'The Atom Smasher'! I follow the thread of thought in his mind, which is literally "Watch out you insignificant little Atoms, The Atom Smasher is coming your way and there is nowhere you can hide and none will survive!... hahaha! (I can even hear

146

the evil laugh)"...far be it from me to be over-sensitive or over-reactive, but I do actually take this rather personally and find myself bristling in response. I have found a child controlling the most powerful and destructive machine on Earth and not only that, this man is a moronic child, with mal-intent, I find myself thinking. How on earth did he get to be in charge, heading up such a significant project? But that was the least of the worries that I came away with, since, as I pass through his mind and his body, but especially his brain, I pick up a severe weakness in the vessels, that is known as an aneurism and he is getting ready to blow. My alarm is extreme, especially imagining this man being the conductor of the orchestra that is about to set sail on a huge experiment, that I know from some of the events that came to pass the last time they ran this machine, had catastrophic effects on the surrounding atmosphere. What might happen this time, if he collapsed at the wrong moment? A perfect storm is brewing. Maybe somewhat rashly, maybe not, I decide to inform Pale Physics Student that his 'boss' is not well on more than one level. I inform him of the super-hero fantasy that is secretly setting this 'Atom Smasher' on fire and even go so far as to paint the exact same visuals in his mind as I had picked up from source and I also unleash the knowledge that this man is not well and that something very, very bad is going to happen in the next month and that he has to be prepared to step up and take over, when the time comes.

He struggles with both bits of information and cannot believe that he has imagined any of it or why. Where on earth did that lot come from, he thinks in the following moments and so I have to reassure him that he has just received an intuitive message that just has to be received and believed and that time alone would reveal it to be true. Trust is what is needed now. I also make sure he has received, deep in his head and his heart, that he is to be the actual super-hero in this situation, who will be stepping up to the plate at the right moment to save the day. No cape required. He chuckles a little to himself, because he's still convinced that this is an idle fantasy of his own construction.

One evening, on the phone to Moody Blonde, he expresses his concerns to her about the precariousness of the situation since he knows that he is treading on thin ice at times with the head of the project and he hopes to be able to support the project to the best of his ability, without falling foul of any delicate egos in the senior team. He also alludes to his concerns for the sanity and health of the project lead, but does not share all of the detail, since he's a bit worried as to which part of his imagination had cooked all of that up! She has no idea just how capable he has become, since becoming privy to the necessary project information, but feels sure of his capabilities and his potential for sensitivity at the same time. She on the other hand has been struggling with being in a new country, a bit weepy at being alone, saved only by the daily short conversations from across the border in English and having to come to terms with studying after quite a long break, in a foreign land and although it is taught in English, she still doesn't understand everything that is being said or expected of her.

So I make a pledge to spend the next week or so on holiday from CERN, with her, to settle her in and translate where there is difficulty in communications and generally help her come to terms with her new life. She, I decide deserves as much help as he is getting, especially since I have high hopes for them both and I certainly don't want her to get left behind.

Getting over the border always makes me feel so insignificant and invisible, which of course I am to the naked eye. No passport needed, nor waiting in line, for me! I watch the border officials checking everyone's papers and giving certain people such a tough time whilst others are virtually waved through. I know from passing through the officials, that although nothing seems to register on the border guards faces, they are thinking, "oh, here comes that

149

nice gentleman who's been coming through here for at least 12 years, every weekday, on his way to work, poor chap having to show me his pass every time, even though he's like an old friend to me now" and yet on the surface, the poor chap is feeling stressed every day because he feels that he has to prove his identity and demonstrate integrity every day of his working life and all he is ever thinking is "I love the weekends when I don't have to go through this ridiculous charade", and "I cannot wait to work for myself, in my own country and then I won't have to suffer this appalling indignity every day". Poor chap indeed, it pains him deeply so I decide to pass on the guards kindly thoughts about him to ease some of the stress a little and both I and the guard notice his body relax just a little and a small smile appears, that does indeed make things better all round. I love the little things.

Once over the border, I head for Moody Blonde's room on the University campus. She was lucky to get that and I have to acknowledge that I did an excellent job the day that I arranged for the accommodations officer to decide to put her into the 'Yes' pile, when deciding who should get one of the few rather lovely rooms that had been built that Summer. She has her own bathroom and a double bed, which makes her feel more like a grown up than the child she feared University would make of her. She had lived independently, for so long, that she was giving up a lot of freedom coming to study again and the little things like a double bed make all the difference. She also only has to share her kitchen with 3 other girls, which means that it is always tidy and clean and that nobody 'borrowed' her milk or bread. She'd shared with guys in rented flats before, on her travels and had given up on ever finding her food where she'd left it.

I wish that I could say that she was pleased to see me, which of course would be ridiculous, but I certainly was pleased to see her. She really is the most elegant and amiable soul, her gentle spirit makes her light in this world. Something about her brings a room to life when she enters and I find myself swooning around her like a love-sick fool. It's easy for me to understand what Pale Physics student likes and loves about her. She is positive, like a fully charged ion or electron, quite attractive to be near. She embodies the best of what I love about physics and chemistry in her physical and chemical perfection. It's just her German that lets her down!

As I arrive she is in the kitchen making some breakfast before she heads off to university for her first lecture of the day. This morning it's a bacon and egg sandwich and a nice strong British cup of tea to get her started. She made sure to bring plenty of tea bags from home, since a decent tea bag is apparently impossible to find almost anywhere on mainland

Europe. As she's busying herself in the kitchen, a fellow kitchen mate comes in and she feels immediately awkward since this girl is only German speaking, but from a very different region than this and her accent is strange indeed and difficult to keep up with. She takes no prisoners when she speaks and her attitude is that since Moody Blonde has come to study in 'her' country, that she should be the one to stretch herself and make the effort to understand her, regardless of how fast she might be delivering her words. Truth be told, she is rather a lack-lustre and boring young woman, who had never been popular at home or at school and the mean streak in her had just grown in line with the incessant and negative cycle that she has set up in her life. So I decide to let Moody Blonde know exactly what the issues are with this young woman, so that she doesn't waste time on her, or believe that she has done anything wrong herself. I also plant the seed that being happy and joyful in the presence of this other young woman is probably the best way to counter her bad mood and thus she does manage to redress the negativity in the kitchen that morning and quite incredibly they manage to find some common ground by singing to a song they both know the words to, playing on the radio, and the spell is broken, never to take grip again. In that positive moment, I still doubt somehow that they are destined to be best friends, but tolerable friends at least is on the cards.

This kitchen encounter immediately changes the way that Moody Blonde is feeling about her day ahead. She begins to see that if she can thaw out the Ice Queen in the kitchen, that she can indeed cope with all the other threshold guardians that have been causing her little moments of undue stress on previous days. So with a positive mind-set, she grabs her bag and steps out into the early Autumn sun. This will be HER path for the coming year. Her step is light this morning and she feels optimistic about the day ahead. She decides to say "güten morgen" to every living creature that she passes and is grateful that people only come along every 50 feet or so, otherwise she would have felt like a lunatic. The very thought that she might have ended up saying "güten morgen" every second, had a crowd come her way, makes her laugh out loud and then smile all the way to her first lecture.

I know from passing through numerous heads as we glide along the street, that these people are thrilled to be greeted by such a beauty, who seems illuminated from within by positive energy and it strikes me that it has nothing to do with me at all, and that this is her light, her energy. She is a being of light with an energy that sits naturally high up the energetic scale, closer to enlightenment than many that I have met. An Angel.

The issue for Moody Blonde is that she needs to build friendships in her class and in her faculty. She is studying Psychotherapy and Neuroscience. It is a very academic department, full of serious and earnest types who are wary of strangers. But she's not just a stranger, she is also a foreigner. Her lecture today is delivered in English and she is not the only English speaking student in the class. What amazes her is that most German students speak perfect English, so what chance for her to develop her German? Apart from with her new kitchen friend!

I decide to pass through a few heads today and encourage them to speak with her in German and I then translate quickly in her mind and help her to respond in sufficiently good German for them to be encouraged, but not so perfect that they go off like a rocket, gabbling indecipherably. I am aware that she will need to cope without me at the end of the week, when I return to CERN for the imminent start-up of the Hadron Collider, so I don't want to set her up to fail as soon as I leave! This morning's induction lecture is about the stresses that the human mind can be subjected to in academic environments and how this can sometimes lead to a loss of confidence, deflection, avoidance and even mental illness and I guess that it is a deliberate warning to them all, not to get the balance wrong nor place themselves in that kind of danger. I know from passing through the lecturers' mind that he lost a student last year and is determined never to let that happen again. I can tell by lunchtime, that Moody Blonde is feeling at ease, there is a definite will in the place for them all to be happy whilst studying and I can see that she will not need much encouragement to settle in, so that her focus can truly be on her work. I pass through her mind in order to deliver the message, to reassure her that everything is going to be alright and that she is going to be a success.

When I pass on through to see how the message is bedding in, she is humming 'Zippadee doo dah' to herself in her head, so I guess I've done a pretty good job already. She's a dream this girl! I love the ease with which I am going to be able to buff this already rather brilliant diamond.

I follow her about all day, like a dog, mainly to get a feel for her life, her situation and how she reacts to what is happening and I can see that she really just wants an education and to belong to a community. She is not trying to be the top of her class, but would like to feel that she has something unique to contribute. The issue, is knowing exactly what that might be. It's difficult enough to find a path through life, but the real knack has to be to find the right path. Anyone could, of course, find an amazingly successful path, as judged by others in their field, or a failure as judged by those same others, but what does anyone's true path look like?

Knowing comes from deep within your very own human heart or your atomic core, depending on circumstances. Each to their own.

Have I always trod the right path.....since the dawn of time? Or have I just been a rather passive observer of matter and life unfolding around me? Lazy Atom. This question weighs heavily on me all day, so I decide that Moody Blonde is indeed treading the right path and on passing through, I see that her decision to go later than most to University was her way of testing out the options and making sure that none of life's usual nonsense, like doing what teachers or parents suggest, was going to get in the way of her making the right personal choice.

Her independence was indeed one of her greatest gifts, well, that and knowing her own mind and connecting with whom she is. I let her know this with some assurance as I pass through, because I know that she is on the right path and that she is a whole and healthy person making a choice from her heart and needs to feel that confidence, to avoid those difficult, dark nights of soul searching, that might otherwise undermine her. She's over one huge hurdle, since finding her soul mate, which is why they can get on so happily with their work and lives. They both know this and the level of respect between them is huge. Independent sorts. Elevating thoughts in a relationship, above the petty imaginings of your partner diving into the arms of another as soon as you are out of the room, let alone the country, allows love to grow. Avoiding the self-inflicted pain and suffering that so many couples put each other through and that makes a heart shrink, is a stout plan. The path of true love can be seamless it seems and wherever you are and whatever you are doing, you are connected to each other with ease. Fear melts away.

From such a solid platform, things can be achieved and life can be gotten on with, removing the necessity for petty oscillations between Love and Hate; Jealousy and Trust; Belonging and Isolation. The list of potential destructive events is endless in the lives of many, who might be less aware. The un-enlightened. My two protagonists have raised themselves above this type of 'soup dwelling' in creating a sovereign relationship in which to thrive. My job is to keep them communicating, up-beat and on the ball.

At the end of the week, I decide that I can leave her now without a worry and so I do just that. Moody Blonde has just come off the phone to her brother who is living in Melbourne and is excited to hear that the gorgeous girl that he met on the banana farm, where he worked, has moved there to be with him and that they have a great room in a house, in which to live and a job in a bar, in which to work. Life is good.

They say a fond farewell, since she is late and then she is off to a bar for a beer with her classmates, where she'll spend the evening laughing and telling jokes, so I fly off up to the very top layer of evening cloud, from where I can see stars and mountains for many miles and then up I go, higher still and over the mountainous border, back to the scary world of insecure scientists and impending doom.

Chapter 21: **The Dark Universe, a very Dark matter**

Who is that, lurking in the shadows of the roadside hedgerows and behind the factory walls, where she hopes that no-one will see her? There is a familiarity in the energy that she is emitting and so I pass through to get an up-close and personal insight into what she is planning. Her mind is full of curiosity and a strong certainty too, that something currently invisible needs to be seen, to be uncovered. Her desire to reveal the hidden and the unseen secrets of the few to the many, is burning like a fire inside. Conversely though, she can keep a secret too when the stakes are high and knows when it is time to disappear, without revealing anything at all. She is like mist.

This snapper of dragon mist, gateways, Orbs and Atoms is a bit of a mystery to me, since even after passing through on numerous occasions, I cannot fathom her motivation. She is as elusive as the energy that she attempts to capture in her digital camera. She is the seeker of truths, both the truths that she needs for herself in trying to tread the true path of her life, but also the truth for others, who need to hear and heed the call to step forward into the light and be counted, to become part of the solution that will save the planet and its people. Not an Eco-warrior she, but following in the footsteps of the guardians and the guides whose hearts are pure and who have guarded the secrets of this planet that are cunningly aligned and buried with the crystal grid and sacred sites that have kept this planet safe and enabled it to survive and thrive for so long. What brings her here I wonder? It's a little odd that she should pop up in so very many places that I have been in recent times! Maybe she's stalking me! I know that she has definitely seen me and captured me even, in that digital lens of hers. I wonder what amazing secrets she has uncovered since last we met and how many of them she has understood and how many more of them she has still to capture and fathom. Unsure why, I am pleased that she is here, since someone has to bear witness to whatever is going on here and capture it for posterity. I pass through her mind to understand her motivation and see that it is pure curiosity and a calling that she received slowly and subtly across the past decade. She had no idea what was happening, when slowly, strange and unexplainable phenomena started to appear in her shots. She met their arrival with faint annoyance, since she was a professional photographer, who didn't need the worry and distraction of having to retouch her work or discard shots with huge blobs in them, but the more she looked and the more she checked her lens for dust and the lights for flaring, she came to realise that this was not a problem and that what she was capturing was in fact a gift and largely a message of hope. She was still in the stage of working out exactly what it all meant and had also found that she was not alone in this adventure. Others were also capturing this material in a range of forms. The difference with her was that she knew she was the messenger and that she had a pivotal role to play in knowing right from wrong when something had to be done. Whatever was behind this, it was coming fast and it was speeding up and gathering malevolent energy as it went.

I know, from passing through, that she had come to CERN to see whether this region had any particular geographical significance, in the way that she has already established that California had and the Cathar region in France, both of which she had connected with in recent and also more ancient times. The building of such a facility here would not have been purely down to there being sufficient space, since arguably it was one of the least likely choices on that score. There had to be another significant reason for that location to have been chosen for such an international and significant scientific facility. She could tell that the energy of the place was very mixed. On the face of things this was a seemingly benign science facility, that invited the public to see it as a part of the forefront of scientific development and a little bit like the Science Museum in London, since it also

161

had a gift shop, but what the public was buying was only what CERN was happy to sell and they had no proper idea of what was really going on here.

Our lurking photographer had decided just to lurk for a bit here, as interested tourists do and capture whatever was around in the ether. She took shots both night and day, all over the area, like a very good tourist indeed. The night shots were more productive, since as soon as dusk arrived they came out to play, the wil-o-the-wisps, the Orbs, the wispy and angelic energies and she suspected that they were in actual fact surrounding her at all times, but that she could only capture them when the flash going off against the darker background would allow them to be seen. Having thought that for a few years now and having spent most of her time in search of twilight opportunities, she had unexpectedly that very morning, started to capture a whole different energy here in her lens, in broad daylight. This was a first! Normally the orbs that she captured were white, or occasionally tinged blue, green or pink, some with recognisable interior structures that were repeated shot after shot and could be attributed to the same re-occuring orbs that appeared regularly in her shots, or with particular familiar people nearby. Today, she had captured her first black orb and what surprised her most, was that it was in the middle of the day, in shiny bright sunlight. It had appeared above the head of one of the passing scientists who had popped out to go to the chemists across the road from the facility. He was a hunched and disgruntled looking individual, who seemed very pre-occupied with his teeth. She took surreptitious shots of all who entered or left the facility across the fortnight that she was there and though she had not captured something every time, was certain that the frequency of capturing something was getting much greater by the hour. Greater than many places in which she had undergone similar clandestine manoeuvres.

The black orb captured today was a first for her and it threw her into confusion, since she had not even heard of their existence before. She had speculated that the orbs thus far were light beings, maybe the souls of the yet to be reincarnated, who were shadowing a loved one, or maybe angelic energy there to protect a subject. It had always been considered positive and light and a good sign, so what was she meant to make of a black one? One with absolutely no light in it at all, almost like the thickest black cloud imaginable, following someone around with extremely bad weather on board. She tracked this scientist every time he left the building, which in previous months would have been rarely this often, but due to his agitation this week, had become a much more regular occurrence. Up to 5 times a day. His sorties often seemed to focus around his

163

appearance, since he first came out to go to the chemist and then after that to the local clothes shops. He seemed to be working quite hard on improving his appearance.

Lurking photographer speculated that maybe there was a female scientist who had recently come to work with him that had woken something up in his world. Sadly that was very far from the truth and she was being far too generous to this largely destroyed and demented man. What was obvious from all of the shots that she took, was that something had attached itself to him, something that could not reside within, but that wanted to be attached so very much, that it hung around above and about, outside of his body, sometimes even outside of the building, maybe over the room that he was working in. It meant him harm.

She had heard of entities attaching themselves to people before, but mostly they dove in deep and made themselves quietly and secretly at home, pretending to be a part of the whole, this one had not been able to do so for some inexplicable reason, but had not given up on trying and so it shadowed him at all times. He felt its presence, I know from passing through and it had destroyed his equilibrium and he had become both frightened and introverted over the time he had been at CERN, whilst trying to stay sane and whilst trying to keep it away. I also know from passing through, that he wears an Obsidian necklace and also carries vast quantities of Obsidian with him at all times, a habit that he had picked up when he'd lived with a rather odd Aunt one Summer in a little wooden house in Iceland. They had gone on endless walks up and down volcanoes, hunting for rocks, crystals and stones and he'd developed a particular liking for the way Obsidian had made him feel safe and so, in later life he had collected and bought a lot of it to add to his collection and it now encircled every area of his world and had unwittingly created a very powerful shield. He had no idea that its protective qualities were a definite match for this dark energy that was following him around, but I know that now. Funny how his instinctive self knew exactly how he needed to keep himself safe. Sadly it had kept out the good as well as the bad and so in many ways he had suffered deeply and personally in spite of it.

He wanted nothing to do with the unexplained or unscientific and there was no way on Earth that he could have mentioned to any colleagues, what had been happening to him, without being hounded from the place that he had worked his whole life to be a part of. They would not entertain employing a self-confessed fruit-loop! He had no friends and could not relate well to his parents and so he was entirely alone with this.

What concerned me also was the possibility that other scientists could indeed have been unwittingly invaded by these black spheres and the lack of Obsidian in their world had made it a synch for them to get on board and bed in for the long haul, waiting for the moment when they needed to take things over. My next job was to pass through a few more of these people in order to ascertain who was a lost cause and who was still safe from this malevolence. I also needed to identify something of the intent behind accessing scientists in this manner and what the possible outcome might be should their plan come to fruition. It occurred to me that this scientific community had a very narrow view of the Universe indeed and that it was only really interested in tinkering, when actually there was a whole much larger universal plan at work that involved absolutely everything that had ever been and that ever would be. They wanted solely to play with the fragments, the bits and bobs and for some reason were almost avoiding the main event. Maybe it was their incapacity to comprehend the infinite possibilities? Blinkered.

If they had suspended their desire or obsession with becoming important specialists in a field of one sort or another and had embraced the whole, The ALL, they might have been able to see the bigger picture, as could I.

I have traveled through space since the dawn of time and I know that The ALL is real and that everything and every one is a part of it whether they know it or not. No-one can deny The ALL and no-one can deny The Nothing either. Existentialists embraced the possibility of this, but were disregarded as depressive, though philosophical types grappling with the unknown. They had surely tapped into that universal energy of everything that was and everything that will be, they just didn't realise how very right they instinctively were. Insufficient scientists, have consciously engaged with philosophy until later in their lives. They sometimes toy with the moral dilemmas faced in certain areas of experimentation, but rarely go beyond that. By paying lip-service to humanity and morality, they feel absolved of any ongoing responsibilities and then just plough on regardless, playing God. Convincing themselves that whatever it is they are being asked to consider has to be factual, pure and simple, or have some basis in fact at least and that everything has to be tested and proven, or dis-proven, by a theorem of one sort or another, in order for it to have any credibility whatsoever and this I am very sad to report will be their undoing! Some things just ARE, without us having the capacity or the need to know 'why'.

My challenge to science is to look above the top of their test-tubes in the lab and to see what they had stopped looking for a very long time ago, which is the actual TRUTH. My second challenge to science is that they engage their intuition also, since they are molecular and very much a part of The ALL that is going on all around them and by tuning into that, they have a very great chance of actually seeing it. Since now I know for sure, that it wants to be seen.

I have a hunger to know about the geographical choice of CERN, since it makes so little sense to have chosen it and so I dive underneath it, deep into the depths of its foundations into the mountainous bedrock of this exceptional finger of Switzerland that juts oddly out of itself and into the French countryside, like an annoying sibling poking its neighbour at dinner to see what reaction it can elicit. I dive in, deep underground, so that I can see what is there. As I pass through, I can see that the circular Hadron tunnel has been buried deep into the ground and know that must have been quite a feat considering the numerous towns and villages that exist in the region. This metal tube, within which the particle accelerator or Hadron Collider is housed, a tunnel that allows particles to be accelerated so very fast that the temperatures created are 100,000 times hotter than The Sun, in fact they create Neutron-star type temperatures when these collisions take place, capable of turning Gold into Iron and Gold into Copper and Lord only knows what into Gold. All alchemical changes are possible in this tubular space. What I also learn, as I pass through, is that if the particles can be accelerated to a sufficient speed, that sufficient powerful negative energy can be created that it can be harnessed and maybe used in a range of potentially rather bad ways.

Physicists believe that they might be able to time travel through a wormhole that might be created in this machine, also known as ATLAS, holding the very fate of the world upon his shoulders and working alongside ALICE, who went down the rabbit hole herself. But what else could happen in this land of such incredible and crazy potential? I pass through the very earth beneath it all and discover something that I can barely dare to acknowledge. I find a chasm of absolute nothingness. The deep, darkness of this nothing sits like the open mouth of a foul and hungry dog from hell, salivating at the possibility that it is about to be let out to hunt for food. A sudden remembrance of an old imprinted image brings itself to the forefront of my awareness. It is the logo for the CERN complex and I realise that it is not spinning orbits of planetary trajectories, nor the interior structure of an atom, but actually it is the 666 of the devil and Hades and everything that is evil in the universe, all rolled up into one simple representation. The un-spun symbol is hiding its intent in plain sight.
In my panic to escape the dread that this black hole reaching into hell has imbued in me, I fly about in a less

than controlled fashion and find myself coming too painfully close to the empty mouth of this gaping whorehole from hell and can hear faint howls and an energetic hunger that is projecting itself out into the centre of the CERN tunnel, trillenia of evil has been locked away in this pit at the centre of the Earth and it has been watching and waiting for the gate to open for such a very long time, that it won't take more than a nano-second for it to leap out once the long awaited moment comes. Maybe some of it has been leaking out for a while and getting itself into pole position, in readiness for the main event? The betrayal that I now feel is complete. These scientists are unwittingly about to harness negative energy and create negative matter in their little experiment, that might open a gateway that will destroy everything that I Love and that I hold dear, they are also about to unleash a hell upon this planet, that will render all life and attempts at survival both hopeless and pointless. Nemesis.

Who will care where, in the world, there is currently a war, or a famine, or a stock market crash, when the gates of hell have opened and let the devils out? I fly out of there as quickly as my little atomic body will carry me, determined to do something to stop this from coming to pass. I need to understand who my allies are and whom I can trust and whom I can call upon to put a stop to this at the right time, so that nobody is in a position to intervene and make sure that this destruction happens after all. My only hope is that I can engage Pale Physics Student as my primary ally and position him unwittingly in the right place at the right time, so that he will react under my instruction and not panic by knowing too much in advance and give himself away and blow the one chance that we have to save everyone and everything that I hold dear on this beautiful Earth. I take a look at the schedules for CERN and can see that there is a technical stop planned for the end of November, followed by a whole month in December where something major is planned to take place, followed by yet another technical stop. Who are they kidding! It won't be so much a technical stop at the end of December, as the end of The Earth as we know it, the ultimate technical stop, a great big FULL STOP!

Chapter 22: **Time Out**

I had always known that I had the potential to get into a rather agitated vibrational state at times, highly strung some might have said. This had previously happened when I was extra happy or super-sad or when I had engaged in a more or less enlightened practice of some sort, or had been deeply influenced by positive or negative situations. I was also aware that I could get angry sometimes when things went badly wrong in my opinion, or when there was a lot of unexpected negativity about. I was also sure that I could recall sometimes getting very angry indeed and that could then lead to more destructive situations that I myself might well have caused, and of which I was far from proud.

The revelations of the last few hours and what I had seen, had taken me to a terrible place and I found myself in such an agitated state that I was a bit worried about what damage I might inadvertently cause. I decided that since there was a full week of technical stop before they started to do whatever it was that they had planned for December, that I would take myself to a place of safety and a place where I could do no damage, could meditate and clear myself of emotion or error, in order to make the right plan and the right decisions at the right time, especially since the future of this beautiful Earth and even the Universe itself depended upon little old 'Me' getting it right. I drifted up, up and away as though in a trance. All I knew for sure, was that I had to leave immediately and not come back until I was calm and equipped with a most excellent plan to implement on my return. So that is what I did.

My chosen destination for time out was The Moon, one of the solar system's younger planets and as Earth's natural satellite, an obvious choice. It has always had such a powerful elemental effect, both being a rousing and a calming influence on everything on Earth. Its ability to create the ebb and flow of the tides on Earth soothed millions of creatures across the millennia and it has a powerful way of enhancing the passions too.

The rock of which the Moon is forged is the same largely, as is found on Earth and its core is iron, as on Earth. It even has a molten core, which I find as I pass through. One of the main differences I also know, is the lack of valuable metals such as Gold and Platinum, that must have landed on Earth long after the Moon was created out of Earth's original raw materials, so the Earth came first and then I know, from passing through, an impact in those early unstable years had literally knocked bits off Earth and sent them flying to form the Moon, its poorer sibling. So man's close connection with the Moon is entirely understandable, since they are fundamentally from the same family. Moon being the younger brother, who didn't get as much attention as brother Earth, nor the rich resources nor the brains of its older sibling and never quite lived life to its big brother's extent. Moon happened to be full on the night that I headed that way and its brilliance was mesmerising, basking in the reflected glory of the other planets. It looked especially fresh, alive and luminescent appearing as it did, from behind the most amazing cloud formations that danced across its face, hiding, then revealing it as if they were playing coquette and lover to each other. The clarity of the moon that night reassured me that I knew what I was doing, so I headed toward it with hope in my heart and a steely determination to calm myself and then plan. Meticulously.

As I arrive on its surface, I can see that it has none of Earth's life-giving properties, but it is not so very dissimilar in its composition or even its innate energetic vibration, coming up from the core. In essence, it is a large grey rock, that has formed out of molten rock and on cooling managed to shape itself into a perfect sphere that has only been blemished since by the huge number of larger and smaller impacts that have delivered an onslaught to it across the millennia, that have left both craters and mountains in equal measure. It feels like an honest sort of a place, with very few secrets and nothing much to hide, unlike Earth right now, which now seems like a complete fraud, with much more dark and shadow than light.

Arriving, I can see that The Moon's surface is pitted all over with craters and rims of varying sizes, I fly all around, taking it all in and can see that what had looked like lakes from Earth are in fact pools of solidified molten larva that has poured out of the core and formed itself flat like glass in the basins of the craters, filling them up. These are of such dense material and I know from passing through that it is mostly Obsidian. This can be no coincidence and I note the strength of the material, due to its molecular density, but also the resistant power of its mass and its ability to repel anything unwanted. It is no coincidence at all that our shambolic scientist at CERN has surrounded himself with this material and I now can see that it had become a necessity for his very survival. He instinctively knew what he needed and I now know too that I might need to find a way to get him to bring it to the Laboratory in quite large quantities, if its protective power is to be harnessed sufficiently to protect the innocents who work there, when things kick off.

On the dark side of The Moon, I find the South Pole Aitken-basin, some 1,390 miles in diameter and over 8 miles deep and feeling safer there than I had back on Earth just before I left, I hide and I rest and I tune out, leaving the worries of The Earth behind me. Here I seek peace and some certainty about the next steps to take. I travel metaphorically in a dream-state recalling the months on Uluru and walk the Shaman path yet again, in search of wisdom, truth and the essential guidance that will get the job done.

In my dreams, I am taken back across time to the point at which Earth was still young and relive the moment when it was hit by a huge planet the size of Mars, which shattered it to such an extent that a lot of its still forming matter was thrown off into orbit just outside its atmosphere, far enough away not to be drawn back down to Earth. I see it magically coalesce into the Moon that I am now sitting upon, though molten to its very surface for many millions of years before cooling sufficiently to form a crust. I witness the bombardment of this satellite of Earth and how it coped and kept itself together. I even witness the temporary establishment of basic life, that sadly could not remain due to the lack of atmosphere and then on to becoming this quite barren Obsidian-hard planet, covered in a powdery layer of grey Moon dust. Not cheese after all. Many life forms have visited here I now know, from connecting with the very

176

inner Iron core of this sphere. It remembers them all, stopping for a rest and looking over at Earth and hopping on over to stake some small claim on the surface of Earth, unbeknownst to most who lived there. We are not alone in this Universe and some life forms have just quietly sat upon the Moon, waiting for the right moment to complete the journey and arrive silently and quietly on the very best of planets, where they have lived safely for millennia. Earth is a shared planet.

In my meanderings I have come to realise that because we are not alone, that there are others with a vested interest in the survival of Earth and its flora and fauna. They might not care so very much for the people, since they are probably Earth's biggest issue these days, but their intention would unlikely be the eradication of the entire human species. They'll manage that for themselves with ease, with their polluting and pillaging ways. But I also know from the wisdom that I receive when passing through, that Earth's visitors come in both positive and negative form. If my understanding of what is incarcerated in that pit under CERN is correct, most of the bad has been rounded up and sealed in there. So maybe the good is still around too, lurking not too far away. Or maybe further up in the wider solar system looking down and keeping a weathered eye on things, or lingering in the spirits of the 'people' that have attached themselves to Earth. Lurking photographer certainly seemed to have identified a range of mostly good energetic phenomena up to this point and now a sudden whiff of the bad, which is in such stark contrast to the good that it is truly shocking. Evil seems to be so much more acid and determined and quicksilver like in its capacity to attack at speed. The gentler nature of good has meant that at times it has fallen victim to its opposite number, but I am hopeful that it has had sufficient time across recent millennia to gather itself and to know how to apply its goodness in such quantities as might prevail in a fight. I might be being naïve or overly hopeful, but I refuse to despair. As I sit and analyse and unpick the situation that I have uncovered back on Earth, I make a mental list of the positive people that I have on the ground on whom I can call. Intuitively, this list comes together and rather unexpectedly, the disheveled scientist is quite high up on that list, just after Pale Physics Student, Lurking Photographer and, of course Moody Blonde. The other surprise entry on my list is the ambitious female scientist and although she appears to be very ambitious and driven, I know that she is in fact an Angel that has lost her way some long while ago and who is looking for an opportunity to absolve herself and help to heal some old wounds caused by her thoughtlessness in the past. I welcome this news, since we are up against some pretty foul energies that will need out-smarting and the more great minds the better as far as I am concerned.

I decide that I must return to Earth, in advance of the operational month in December and hook all of these people up, so that there is an allegiance and a subliminal knowing that can be called upon when the moment comes and they all have to be prepared to act without hesitation. I am also very aware that I will have to work very hard indeed at briefing them individually to make sure that they will act like perfectly attuned machinery against the scheming mass of blackness that has had millennia to plan and make allegiances. Their attack will be ruthless in the chaos that will be created and could throw the average human completely off their focus, but I will have planted an army-like plan in their heads and have them fully drilled in its choreography, to make sure that chaos will have absolutely no power in the situation, come the day. I will have to rely somewhat on the possible complacency of these malevolent beings, maybe in the assumption that they might well have made, that they are about to win this imminent battle, since they have been planning it forever and also the hope that they have not picked up on my involvement in masterminding Earth's defence. They cannot see me or the part that I have been playing, I represent the element of surprise, which is a major advantage. Atoms have never been of interest to them I now know, having connected with that foul energy under CERN the other night. They are obsessed with flesh and blood, since they have mistakenly decided that this is what makes men and women who they are, which cannot be farther from the truth. I know from passing through that what truly makes man special is his ability to rise above all of that. I also know that though I might only be an Atom, I know with certainty what the best and worst of humanity looks like and yes, it is flesh and blood, but this is coupled with an intelligent energetic life force and an endless capacity for Love. Beyond flesh into the higher realms of Universal love, connecting humanity to the purest energies that have been created, transcending bodily obsessions, connecting humans to The ALL.

My list of 'potential saviours' gets backed up by a list of 'resources required', which is topped by Obsidian and then White lab coats, followed by Passes into the secure areas of the facility, for both Moody Blonde and Lurking Photographer. They have no idea that they are about to play a pivotal role in saving 'absolutely everything' and really are only thinking about their immediate personal landscape or the current research mission that they might be on. These drivers alone are sufficient to keep them focused on being near CERN when I need them, so I am satisfied with that.

The other thing that I realise, which sends a nasty energetic shudder through my little Atomic body, is that I need to pay another visit underground to check out what is afoot and how these evil things might be preparing themselves in advance of the assault. The worst of this realisation is that I will have to travel deeper than before, into the very foul mouth of this cave of horrors in order to ascertain what my heroes and heroines are actually facing. I doubt that I will ever have witnessed such things before, since they have not freely roamed Earth since they were locked away at the very formation of this planet, locked in its very iron core. Something tells me that they might not have managed to capture every last bit of malevolence at that early time, which would account for the very many bad things that have happened across time ever since, but the overall balance has been kept in favour of good not evil and the events that are imminent will doubtless tip that balance very much in the wrong direction and will potentially be somewhere very dark, from which it is not possible to recover. I prepare myself, as best I can, with a meditation that takes me up to the highest vibrational state that the Universe can support and I meet with white light, filled with such pure love that I bask in it for a whole 48 hour period until I am brimming over with it. I am so very bright, that I am a little concerned that it will affect my invisibility, since I am shining as the purest diamond would, if it were filled with love.

Chapter 23: **Knickerbockerglory**

It started like almost any other day. Though it was clear to me that nothing that happened on this day would be normal, nor necessarily end particularly well. The Path in Sussex had a slight mist lingering on it this morning as the first two of the morning runners came along it, at the side of the wood. Unusually it was Froufrou out, looking rather eager, who was following a young man well into his stride already. She had been noticing him a lot on The Path and fancied that this morning, it was time to get his attention, so she ran after him as fast as she could manage and then deliberately fell down just behind him squealing in agony in an attempt to get his attention. She was visibly shocked however, to see that he just kept on going without even so much as a turn of the head, or any concern whatsoever. She was filled with immediate rage and frustration, in that instant, since she had been convinced that this melodramatic act played out upon The Path would get her noticed, or elicit a little sympathy at least. All it got her was bloody knees, a bruised right buttock and hurt pride when the young man, unaware and listening to Bruce Springsteen at high-volume on his i-pod, went jogging off quite oblivious, to the other end of The Path.

Crunch, crunch, crunch, turn the corner once. Crunch, crunch, crunch, turn the corner twice. Well, maybe there is a benevolent and kindly god somewhere, after all, who has decided to take pity on poor Froufrou, since the heroes come along The Path towards a damsel in distress with bloody knees and hurt pride and they do indeed stop and make a proper fuss of her in the early morning mist, since she is probably 20 years younger than each of them and they rather like to feel that they are each both gentlemen and saviours rolled into three rather amazing bodies. One has a first aid kit in his small backpack and is always ready for an emergency, so they patch her up and send her on her way and she feels a little better for having been made a fuss of, which was all she had really wanted, after all!

Crow Man was standing in his field at the top by the wind blasted trees, surrounded by more crows than even he had ever seen. They cawed at him as though they were complaining that something wasn't right today and that it was up to him to pass the message on, or to advise them, in his wisdom, as to what needed to be done. He both heard and felt the jarring energy in their calls, but knew nothing of the world of which they spoke and could not possibly know whom to call or what necessary course of action to set in motion that would do anything at all to change the situation. He tried to calm them with his usual words, but that had no

183

effect. Then from a place deep inside himself, came rising up a powerful desire for self-expression that he hadn't felt ever before and he tapped into something unexpected or maybe just long forgotten, which rose up from deep in his body and he started to sing.

He had no conscious memory of the song that he sang, since in this body he had never sung it before, but the memory of it came from long ago and resonated in his old bones as he chanted the warning song of the Mimbrenos Indians of Southwestern New Mexico, who wandered the banks of the Gila River deep in the Gila Wilderness where Geronimo came to hide and where they had lived in peace and harmony for centuries, until the white man came and everything had changed for the worse. He hummed and chanted this song to the Crows that surrounded him and they heard the message that they were indeed right to be concerned, for something was coming that wanted to destroy everything and that their job was to pass the message on from Crow to Crow and to engage the Magpies too and all the other long range birds to take a message out across the world, that trouble was coming out of Switzerland and that they needed to get ready for a fight.

The message went out that the trouble would come from below, from deep in the darkest and most evil places in the very core of the planet and that they should be able to recognise good from evil by its energetic intent, which would be very clear indeed. They sent instructions that destruction of these negative energies was the only option and that they should not hesitate in taking swift action to terminate these creatures as they swarmed malevolently across the surface of the Earth.

At CERN the lead scientist most oddly decides that he fancies an ice-cream before the real business of the day starts. He decides that he has earned it and he also remembers that his grandmother had said that he could not have any rewards until he had not only completely finished his work, but proved that it was indeed so. He had always felt that he was not good enough in the rather critical family in which he was raised, governed by two very powerful women. So today of all days, since he was planning on playing God today and since he was the one in charge, not those nasty old women, that he was going to treat himself to an extra large Knickerbockerglory before the work of the day began.

He came into the facility extra early this morning, just to check up on everything and to see that all of his orders issued to his team the evening before had indeed been carried out to his precise specification, since he had left a little early yesterday to indulge in a visit to the Grand

Théâtre de Genève to see Die Fledermaus by Johann Strauss II. He is still musing in his mind over the flirtatious nature of the performance between the three main characters and wishing that he could have been on that stage himself, all dressed up in costume, with the crowd clapping and cheering him on at the end of each act.

Of course Pale Physics Student had meticulously led the team in carrying out every one of his wishes, to the very letter and he looked with some pride at the readiness of the situation. He had a strong and obedient team that he felt every confidence in. He was at last pleased with the way that his newest recruit had made his project even more professional than he could have imagined some three months ago. Contented with the perfection of the set-up, he slipped out of the laboratory and through the many corridors until he got to an exit tucked away at the side of the building, in order to not be witnessed leaving, by any of his team who would soon be arriving for the morning shift.

Down the Route de Meyrin he slides, in search of his guilty pleasure. Knowing that this is wrong on so many levels and only doing it to prove a point to himself, which is that he really is in charge. What he doesn't seem to appreciate though, is that sneaking out the side door and off to his favourite ice cream parlour proves nothing other than to acknowledge his guilt in acting this way and reinforces the incredibly sneaky nature of the act and the knowledge that he really should be more mature than to be behaving in this manner. If he were truly a confident man in charge of his own destiny, the predominant creative force in his life, he would be taking the whole team out for a Knickerbockerglories and getting them jointly into the team mode that he should have been wanting to create.

He is salivating as he enters the Parlour and watches intently with his tongue literally dripping out of the right hand side of his mouth in an unconscious engagement in the visual spectacle of the building of this magnificent glass of ices. He watches as the fresh raspberries and very ripe mango are layered into the seemingly endless scoops of the very finest locally made vanilla ice cream. There are also a generous number of blueberries dropped in around the edges as they build the mixture up through the glass and sprinkle icing sugar and coarsely chopped pistachios throughout. Finally topping the whole thing off with fresh cream and raspberry sauce so that it drips down through the gaps in the layers like backwards flowing magma returning to the heart of a volcano. He pays 20 Swiss francs for this pleasure, but knows that it will be worth every cent. As the woman behind the counter takes his money and passes the ice cream across the counter towards him, anyone watching might have seen a 6 year old boy before them, not the most powerful man on Earth today.

I watch as he savours every last drop of the incredibly cold ice cream and though he is conscious of time, he does try not to rush, but a rush is inevitable, since it was a very large ice cream indeed and he has to get back for a precisely timed and planned start, when his team would be expecting him to deliver instruction. So he does in fact have to rush the last third, but feeling entitled and a very greedy boy indeed he still finishes every drop before rushing out of the Parlour and into the street where he finds himself running back towards his big day and the inevitable brilliance of his powerful experiment. But in his head, he is not running, he is flying in a golden cape, with his little winged golden ankle boots on, with an Atomic 'A' emblazoned across his chest, flying in the air just above chest height to deliver the mighty blow to the atoms that have proved themselves so uncooperative thus far.

The run was not a good idea at all...not the best start to this particularly important day. He makes it though, with minutes to spare, for the planned 9.30am team meeting, where he will be talking through all the checks with the team and making sure that everyone is in place for the start. He is feeling very full now and the coldness that his stomach

188

is grappling with alongside the bulk of the amount that he has just consumed is actually nothing compared to the brain freeze that is taking up its place in his skull. Brain freeze cannot be a great start to a day of this importance...

Pale Physics student had a strange text message this morning from Moody Blonde. She says that she will see him at lunchtime and that she will be on time and in position, as requested and he cannot for the life of him fathom why she is coming today, of all days, to CERN, for lunch! She surely remembers that today is 'The Big Day,' when it all kicks off and he has to be focused on supporting the project and making his mark in this team, so that they will keep him here for the foreseeable future at least?

What he does not know, is that I sent her the text from his phone, begging her to come urgently, since she will be needed at lunchtime at the latest and that she should be ready at the side door that leads out onto the Route de Meyrin, where she can be sneaked in when she is required. She was mighty confused by the message and has absolutely no idea why he needs her, but she trusts him implicitly. She got up as soon as the text arrived at 6am and without question, jumped on a coach across the mountains and the border that separates them, ready and willing to do whatever had to be done. She is naturally disturbed and
189

speculates all the way. In one instant she imagines that it might be a spontaneous romantic liaison that he is planning, when he's at the peak of the thrill of working the Hadron Collider, but she dismisses this seedy thought as soon as it arrives, since that would represent an ego that he simply doesn't possess.

He has turned his phone off since then, as they have a strict no-phones policy in the lab, which everyone adheres to and he arrived at work seconds after the lead physicist had popped out for his icy breakfast. Nothing can be allowed to disturb them when they are at work, so her journey to him is in silence and full of unanswered questions and excitement. Pale Physics Student has run all the technical checks that he knows are necessary before the machine is switched on this morning. He has wandered around the machine room helping colleagues to finish their work too and just generally being his usual helpful self. He slept like the dead last night, which surprised him hugely, since he's normally nervous and excited the night before any major event. But I made sure to send him off into a very deep sleep indeed, by humming in his ear the deep vibration of a meditation that I learned far away on Uluru, that will have taken him to a soulful and deeply nourishing land, where his dreams will have been the purest and capable of touching the deepest places in his good heart, in readiness for the trials ahead. So he is perky, alert and very clear-headed this morning, which I am extremely pleased to note. I also did quite a lot of seed-planting in the night or in the wee hours of the early morning, with sufficient time for assimilation by each of my carefully chosen allies and now we are about to complete on my week of Moon-planning and bring it forth into the light, back here on Mother Earth. My disheveled scientist with no friends or family that he can remember has awoken with an absolute and clear determination that he needs to bring all of his collection of Obsidian into work. He cannot fathom quite why, but tells himself that it will produce a protective force-field of some sort, maybe enhancing or reducing the effect of interference from that bloody Hadron Collider, when it is running today and therefore allowing him to carry on with his work undisturbed. In a way he is right, so not a stupid man on any level. He has spent that early morning boxing it all up and putting it onto his big wheeled trolley with four plump and bouncy wheels, freshly pumped, that will prevent it being damaged whilst crossing over the cobbles of the road and yet small enough that he can pull it through the streets between home and the lab. He is quite pleased with himself at having thought of this solution as he had been feeling a mounting tension in him all week and was not entirely clear what that was about, but decided that it was his concern over the effects of the Collider running, on his own corner of research, which he held so dear. He was

191

endlessly pleased to have come up with such a neat and practical solution.

The other seed that I planted over night, was in the mind of Lurking Photographer, since she was the one witnessing so many energetic phenomena across the globe, that others had not yet seen, nor dared to acknowledge nor bring them out of shadow and into the light. She has been brave. She has been capturing the truth in her lens and it is so very important that if we manage to save the day today, that she has evidence to share with the world, with the governments of the world and more importantly, with every citizen of Planet Earth, who have the right to know the truth of the danger that they have been subjected to. The irony is not lost on me, that by the end of today, that not a single person on Earth might actually care about what just happened here, if they find themselves grappling with the omnipotent terror that will doubtless be surrounding and consuming them if I get this even a bit wrong. She has also been told, by me passing through in the early morning as she lay cosy in her hotel bed, to be at the side door of the CERN laboratory by midday, with her camera, where she will meet a blonde Angel of about 20, whom she should introduce herself to and whose side she should not leave. She is completely flummoxed by waking up with the clarity of this certain message in her head, but is a trusting sort with a genuine attachment to universal energy and messages from above and so just accepts that her time has at last come, when she will be doing something of true worth that will fulfill a major part of her destiny. She always knew that she had a role to play and had been following her instincts for a decade now, in pursuit of the answers that now wanted to be uncovered. Her path had led her here, to this moment. The Lead Physicist walks in with his white Lab coat on and his super-duper clip board in hand, but still panting from his run through the streets back to the lab. His team notice that he is not calm and that he has beads of sweat pouring out from across his whole face. Someone asks him if he is all right and he snaps aggressively back at them, which shuts them all up in an instant. None will dare to question him now that they can see the sort of mood he is in. He's a pretty ugly sort at the best of times, but this mood is very much worse than they are used to. They put it down to his likely tension around getting today to run smoothly and getting this machine running at full tilt by lunchtime, without a hitch. They have no idea that he is now feeling sick in his stomach and his head is aching like a very nasty hangover after a night of drinking and he is also feeling a bit guilty at his stupidly arrogant self-indulgence.

Our disheveled scientist is outside the Lab, chatting happily away to himself and congratulating himself on his brilliant idea, whilst laying out his Obsidian collection in a huge circle right in the very centre of the ground above the Hadron Collider ring, just under where the electrified donut cloud has been gathering every time the machine has run in the past, in the hope that he can counter its creation and cause less disturbance to the similar creation he is making on a smaller scale in his portable weather machine, in the Lab. He seems to like portable equipment that can be trolleyed about. "have trolley, will travel", he is saying to himself, as he happily remembers his somewhat eccentric meanderings to work this morning.

They all know their jobs in the Lab, so they busy themselves with getting on with them. It is 9.35 a.m. on a Tuesday in December and time to run through the final double-checks and then into the countdown. I am in the Lab waiting at the side of Pale Physics Student, not entirely sure what to expect next. He gives them the "5,4,3,2,1, Atom-Smash", which he had always thought very amusing, but the team had thought rather immature, but it is thus today and off they go! The first button is pressed by him, followed by a lever across the other side of the console, pressed by another senior colleague and then another button, to be pressed by Pale Physics Student in synchronisation with another colleague across the room.
There is a gentle hum in the room that rises in volume and vibration as it starts to send power into the Collider. The
194

plan this morning is to warm it all up by getting up to full speed and then stop momentarily to make sure that all seals are holding and then shut it all up again and carry on to full power, keeping it that way for a whole month. The warm-up completed, they bring the machine back to a temporary stop. I pass through the mind of the lead scientist, to check how things are going on in there and realise that the ice-cream has had a catastrophic effect on his aneurism and that it is bulging through the wall of the vein, which has become so pale and thin that I know that he is going to explode at any moment.

I am so shocked that I decide to let my hero know what is about to unfold and he goes across to try and see whether he is alright, or whether he would rather stop for the day. He cannot believe that such words come out of his mouth and the reply he receives is unrepeatable, shocking our hero into submission, wishing that he had not opened his mouth after all.

But he has opened it and he also knows that he is right to have spoken. He tries to explain to a fellow scientist just what is going on, who looks extremely confused that he could be thinking along those lines at all. So it all continues along in this manner, towards its inevitable and disastrous conclusion from that point forward. At the point at which it really kicks off, I reach a dawning and dreadful realisation, that I have absolutely no choice but to join the throng of fellows inside the Hadron Collider.

It is not what I would have wished for myself, or for the planet, since I am an Atom of peace at
my very core, but I have been left with very few options by the time we arrive at this terrible moment. If I'd had tear ducts I would have cried my little atomic eyes out, but I don't. All I have is energy and a huge amount of it and if truth be known, I am getting fucking cross about the situation! I throw myself at the entrance to the machine and manage to gain entry just before it closes tight shut and I know that there is no escape for me now.

The machine starts up again with the same process of button pressing and lever pulling as before, it goes up and up and up to top speed where it starts to hum at quite a heavy and deeply resonant vibration that lacks the lightness of the higher vibration that I would have preferred.

I find myself inside the crazy tube whizzing around almost as fast as I can normally cross the Universe, but actually not quite as fast as that, just yet. I feel that they must surely increase it up a notch at some point. They do, and as things start to travel at the speed of light, I can see Atoms smashing into each other and being sacrificed on the pointless pyre of scientific experimentation. I find that I am faster than them all and more agile, able to avoid every atom and particle that comes my way and in spite of the speed, I am able to recognise some of them from the earlier gathering in the corridor the other day. I also note a new Atom, whom I have never seen before, but inside, when I see it, there is a deep and resonant recognition. It alarms me hugely and I find myself obsessing as to what it might be and as I spin at incredible velocities, I am looking for its form in the whizzing throng.

Pale Physics Student is still a bit shaken by being shouted at, but has regained his equilibrium sufficiently to position himself close to the lead scientist, in readiness for what he needs to do, when something goes wrong, whatever that might be and he has absolutely NO idea what that might be. Deep in his head and his heart, he now knows that he is to be the one, who will be stepping up to the plate at the right moment, to save the day, the team, the equipment and the project, but the craziness of these thoughts is also deeply disturbing to him.

Outside the Lab, disheveled scientist has completed his positioning of Obsidian and he is pleased with the result, especially since he can now feel the vibration coming up through the earth beneath him and into his knees. Large groups of dark birds are gathering on the rooves of the surrounding buildings and they are all looking at him curiously. There is a faint reminiscence of the discomfort that he has been suffering a lot of recently, but he manages to shake it off. He stands up and the vibration from below comes up through his feet, through his whole body and off through the top of his head and out into the Universe. He happens to step into the circle to move one of the stones and is thrilled to find that no such energetic transference is happening from within it, so the obsidian is in fact working 100%. It is keeping the energy away from gathering itself in hugely powerful donut-shaped waves that draw everything up from below and belch it out into the atmosphere. He has stemmed the flow of that energy. Happy with the result, he wanders back towards the side entrance to the building, just as it is approaching midday. Moody Blonde has been standing at the side entrance, as instructed, since about 11.30, not knowing what to expect, but determined not to move from her post. As she stands there, a middle aged woman wanders casually towards her and she introduces herself, saying that she has been instructed to find her here and to stick with her whatever happens, so they fall into easy conversation, since they both recognise each other from The Path that they have both trodden before and know so well back home in Sussex.

198

Their conversation very quickly becomes more urgent when they realise that they have been drawn here by a power much greater than themselves and that they have a very important part to play in something that has yet to reveal itself. Lurking Photographer shows Moody Blonde some of the images that she has been capturing in her camera across the past fortnight and explains about the difference between light Orbs and Black Orbs and that she has a very grave concern indeed about the mental state of some of the scientists that she has been shadowing. She explains that she innately knows that she is both witness and messenger in this situation and will be doing whatever she can to record events so that the truth can be revealed when necessary. She is aware of how vulnerable she feels, but cannot walk away from this place without doing the job that she was brought here to do.

Moody Blonde listens intently, unsure what any of this means. She had never imagined that such a well-known scientific establishment could be at the heart of any kind of dark controversy, especially with so many eminent scientists involved in it and with global oversight and involvement for reassurance. If it were dangerous, surely they would have built it on The Moon, or in a far off desert somewhere in Australia, away from people, villages, indeed the very heart of Europe. This country is so completely surrounded and entirely land-locked and it has 5 nosy neighbours, surely they would all have something to say if they thought that this work posed any kind of threat to its citizens? As they are sharing what they each know, a very dishevelled scientist comes their way and is about to enter the door at which they stand like sentinels. Lurking Photographer recognises him as the very scientist about which she was just speaking and she is mightily confused when he opens it up with a pass key that he has around his neck, combined with a few buttons pressed on a key-pad and then without batting an eyelid, he turns to face them and invites them in. He explains that he's not sure why, but deep inside he has an innate understanding that they are needed inside and he thinks nothing at all about the security implications. He knows that today is like no other. As they all enter the corridor, the lights come on automatically due to the movement and he opens a cupboard door on the inside wall and pulls out 2 white lab coats for them each to put on. He then starts off down the corridor, and without looking back, he is beckoning them with one finger popped rather cheekily over his left shoulder at them, and they follow. He takes them to the Hadron Collider Laboratory entrance and knocks on the door and as they peer in through the glass of the door and almost without them noticing, he simply disappears to get on with his own work.

The inevitable is at last happening in the Lab. The Lead Scientist has turned a funny colour and is swaying a little. He is a mixture of ashen white and boiling red, depending where you looked upon his face. He shudders and yelps and swoons seemingly at the same time and then collapses completely onto the console, setting off every kind of alarm that you can imagine. The machine speeds up and starts to shudder. There are noises in the machine's engine that no-one has ever heard before, there is also instant fear in the room.

These people are not trained in disaster management. Now is when they need the training and military precision of the three from The Path, but they have none of those skills. All they have standing between them and meltdown is a very level-headed young man, who has had a most excellent nights sleep, who steps forward and pulls the scientist off from the equipment and lays him gently to one side. He taps a colleague on the arm and asks that he open the door to the lab and allow the emergency services to come in when they get here from the local Hospital and another he asks to call them urgently. This unstable individual dealt with for now, he turns to the console in front of him and starts to take control back, if he can. What he does not know, is that it might already be too late, since the beasts below have been sufficiently encouraged and the pot of boiling evil is about to spill up and out of the underworld, into the daylight above. Its seething and amorphous dark shape of twisted and depraved form, starts to lift up and out of the mouth of the hell-hole that Atom had seen just a week ago, but finds that mostly it is pushed back down by what can only be described as a force-field of impenetrable black power. The Obsidian is capable of holding it at bay for a little while at least and the confused mass backs off momentarily, to try to work out what has changed from before. Some small wisps of evil do leak out largely unnoticed and slide away from the Lab, out through the open door and up into the morning sky. The sentinels on the surrounding rooves bear witness to their arrival in the good fresh air of Earth today and they fix them in their sights and pursue them wherever they go, taking them out of action by subsuming them deep into their bellies and sacrificing their own lives in the process. Their fellow birds momentarily pay their respects to the fallen and continue on with their own search, determined to leave none at large by nightfall.

At this moment, when the door to the room opens, Moody Blonde and Lurking Photographer fall into the Lab. One with her camera poised and ready to snap away at whatever might appear before her and the other in search of her partner, anxious to know that he is safe. Our Photographer has already picked up on a mass of Black Orbs bubbling up most unusually through the very floor on which they stand. She knows from experience that she is the only one that would be aware of this, since she is only able to see them through her camera, but others in the room are certainly feeling very much outside their comfort zone in the current situation as the energy becomes dark and oppressive and everyone starts to feel a sickness rising. They start to scatter as the door to the Lab opens. They cannot stop themselves from heading straight for the open aperture and running for their lives. Many never look back and few will ever return.

As Moody Blonde heads straight for her partner, she can see that he is entirely in control, as far as he is able, trying to bring the machine back under control, so that he can shut it down.

Whatever happened when the Physicist hit the decks, he jammed some of the buttons down and there was no easy way of levering them back up again or reversing what the pressing of them had set in motion. She could see dark shapes coming up from the other side of the huge machine and the blackness of the energy emanating from them made her violently sick, it was such the antithesis of the positive energy that she was made of. Regaining control, she begins to concentrate every positive thought in her body towards combating the hideous black spew that was now trying to escape from below. She focused on combating the sickness from the inside, with positivity and the brightness of her inner light grew, filling every inch of the room, pouring into every crevice and forcing the dark to retreat once again. Revealing the unknown power within herself and showing it to Pale Physics Student. Like an outpouring of love and light into the space, so powerful that it made him turn. He cannot quite believe the vastness of her power in that moment and is so deeply grateful that she is here, as between them, they manage to hold back the night that would otherwise have swallowed them whole. But in spite of making some positive progress, the fight is not yet won and the battle continues.

Inside the Collider, I am racing forth, in search of my Twin. I have no idea whether we will meet again, but I have to keep trying. My last clear thoughts in this hell-raising tube are one's of absolute resolution and determination. Hell will not break loose into this beautiful Earth and destroy those that I love and I shout out in my rage "I am here, there and everywhere, I've been here since the dawn of time and will be here to the bitter end and the rate you're going, it will be a very bitter end indeed." My anger at these scientists who would play God is so great, that I cannot contain my rage and frustration. "Don't try to crush me, bend me, shape me, I am in my most perfect form and if you put me under too much pressure, I'll go off like a bomb....An Atomic Bomb!!"

I have no idea whether seeking union with my Twin is the solution or will be the ultimate end of The Earth, but something inside tells me that there is good in us both and that nothing bad ever came out of an act of absolute Love between two good things and so, I fly forth in an ever more determined search. And with that I go super-sonic and I reach speeds faster than the speed of light and focus my attention on the end result of colliding only with my twin, whom I know for sure has the exact same desire.

In the very next nanosecond we see each other in the atomic flow and deliberately collide and absorb each other entirely, but instead of reacting and causing the second Big Bang and finding the elusive Higgs Boson, or God particle, we just find each other and the whole crazy thing comes to an immediate yet soft halt. In less than a second everything that had welled up from that hell-hole beneath, fell back down, down, down into the pit from which it had risen and there was a strange hush as a vacuum of sorts was suddenly created, sucking them back in. It was over.

Chapter 24: **The Wisdom of Atom**

The air was fresh and clear and the sky seemed supra-luminescent, pouring determined beams of light down from an even more determined Sun, into the darkest recesses of every part of the World.

At the side of the wood The Sun poured out light from its low position in the sky, across the immaculate golf course, with its tightly cropped green and sunlight relished gently touching with green-gold brilliance the very tips of each blade of long, languid grass. The gentle breeze sent every stem into a subtle backwards and forwards gyrating motion that sent a soft vibration up through the morning air and out into space.

All is well with The World today, though it could so very easily have been a very different scene this morning. There may well have been nothing but foul black and pain, but instead there is light. The oblivion of each passing runner, walker, golfer, shrew, mouse and vole is a blessing on this beautiful morning. We pass through this scene with such gratitude that these people, these simple creatures have been spared the knowledge that would certainly have destroyed their sanity, had their bodies survived that dark day back in early December.

We survey this scene with gratitude, my twin and I, the twin that I found at last under Sagittarius in the early days of December, at polar opposites to Gemini on the Astrological chart. We found each other against the odds and now that we are One, we are both at peace in this magnificent Solar system. We both have tales to tell each other and millennia in which to recount them. We also both have a story about what led us both to each other in that fortuitous moment in the Hadron Collider, since we were both led there by a force much greater than our own, the Wisdom of the Universe was in charge in the run up to that. We are content, we are whole.

That day passed in a blur of anxiety and energetic determination, focused on the end result of everyone living through it, to draw breath once again the following morning and for it to be History. A story to tell....rather than a prison sentence about to commence.

The creatures of the Earth are free for now, free from being consumed by the putrid hate that had been swarming like an evil soup below Geneva, since the formation of Earth, awaiting its moment of dreadful glory and the destruction of everything good. Evil sealed into the molten heart of such a beautiful planet, masking its dreadful secret with its outward abundance and beauty, from being known to all for what it is. Maybe such beauty, such good, is only possible as an antidote to something as dread as that. The contentment I feel today is absolute. My twin and I reflect on how privileged we are to bear witness to the simplicity and beauty of life on Earth, when evil is not burgeoning forth. On The Path we see some regulars, whose lives have not been touched by this experience at all, though they do just seem to be alright, where maybe they were a little less than content before. Maybe that is sufficient reward for what we have experienced.

I see Crow Man intersecting The Path halfway up, as he often does, coming to feed his crows, walking slowly and as if to a rhythm within, he is hesitant as the beat changes, but I can see that there is repetition in his movements as he almost sambas up the meadow. I can feel the radiant joy of his inner contentment. His granddaughter has just given birth to her first child and he is musing over their choice of name for her, which is Kitty. Such a delightful name for such a delightful and perfect little human being. He joked at the naming that she would be an Atomic Kitty, since she never slept and he will always call her that and she will always love him for it. The Crows, as ever, are pleased to see him, with his bag of scraps and the gentle humming of an endless stream of Mimbrenos Indian chants that come through him, from he knows not where, but have brought with them a contentment and an intuitive link to the wisdom of this old man and those ancient Indians of the American North West.

Passing along The Path at a gentle pace, comes Froufrou, who seems to have developed a maturity that was sadly lacking before. She has started reading books and articles, which is a massive departure from the norm for her and has stopped being so obsessed with how she looks and who might fancy her today. Brought about seemingly, by her meeting a handsome young man in the coffee shop, where she works in town, which seems to have woken her up. The realisation that she can be great friends with a gorgeous man and the rewards that this brings her has been somewhat of a revelation. Following up on their conversations and writing down details on her notepad behind the counter, she has been quietly seeking out the books that he has mentioned, reading them and then starting to engage in more meaningful conversations with him and many other customers besides. She likes owning knowledge, since it has opened up a whole world of possibility to her and she is gaining satisfaction in so many new ways these days. I feel hugely satisfied that she has come to this place of contentment on her own, since I would never have predicted that.

Redhead overtakes Froufrou, with a very handsome man at her side. He reminds me of the warriors of old, with an amazing chest and long, flowing blonde locks and I see that they both have their hair loose as they fly past in a state of wild abandonment, laughing and joking with each other. The energy that they carry with them is full of sexual tension, high excitement and early signs of love. They are a sight for sore eyes indeed.

We see other familiar faces along The Path and drift away from it to check up on our heroes and heroines, who are not living in these parts these days. Lurking Photographer has had a tough time of it in the aftermath of that day at CERN. She captured some incredibly disturbing images in her lens and was filled with a deep fear as soon as she knew what she had. It was obvious to her that she was in imminent danger, should she go public with any of this, or should anyone realise what she had been up to. The building of this facility, at this location was no coincidence, so somebody in a position of huge influence would have known of its true purpose and since their intent was so deeply evil and destructive in nature, she had to hide her evidence, her camera and even herself, if she was to ever get out of there in one piece and bring the truth of the situation out into the light in personal safety. We knew that she was really the most vulnerable of all, of the heroes of the hour and took it upon ourselves to protect her from their mal-intent. She had certainly been followed from the moment she left the facility, indeed she might have been followed inside of it, but we could not have known that since we were still locked up inside the Collider for at least an hour after it all cooled down and we might never have escaped its confines, had not Pale Physics Student decided to open it up out of curiosity, to see what was going on inside. He had to check that it was indeed over, for once and for all, before he could draw a line under it and move on with his life.

Moody Blonde was still in a trance-like state in the immediate aftermath of events, while he opened up the sealed door and let us all out. He felt the energy pass through the air around him and in a massive show of absolute respect, none passed through him, since he had been one of the saviours of the day, Earth and life as we have grown to know and love it. He felt caressed by loving energy as they stroked his face and body and moved back out into the world to fully appreciate that they had a future to engage in. Many had died that day, smashed to pieces by 'The Atom Smasher's' device, hurling them at their brothers and sisters and they wanted no part of it anymore. They wanted light and warmth and the energy of love, whilst living out their long atomic days at the very highest vibration.

Atoms and particles dispatched, things normalised surprisingly quickly. Now that pure evil was shut back deep underground, Pale Physics Student took it upon himself to remove some fundamental pieces of the machine, that would render it useless for a while at least. He knew that he could not defeat evil, permanently or single-handedly. It had to come from the positive will of mankind as a whole, to make sure that these hideously corrupted, shadowy and powerful people, who lurk somewhere behind these huge organisations, these Puppet Masters, could be thrown up into the clear light of day and revealed in all their putrid glory.

He would need Lurking Photographers' help, he knew for sure, but was not naive enough to imagine that she would want to be so exposed. Neither would he. He crossed the Lab towards her and took her by the arm in a reassuring manner and slipped his details into her hand and spoke clearly into her ear. He told her to leave as quickly as she could manage, to put herself and her images somewhere safe, where no-one would know to look and to contact him once she had done that, with some coded message that he would work out and that he would come and find her and that they would plan the next step. With that message softly ringing in her ears, he pushed her gently towards the Lab door and she fled. The Mistress of seeing the unseen proved also the Mistress of being unseen and she went to stay with old friends in the Cathar region of France, where she knew that she would be safe for a while at least, since they had kept many secrets there, for many centuries and she knew that they kept them still.

At her departure, he had turned to the woman at his side and opened his arms sweeping her up into a loving embrace that they both needed in that moment. The tension that they had both been holding for months now, just slipped away and neither spoke a word for a very long time. Grateful to be alive and together at this post-apocalyptic moment, when things could have turned out so very differently. We witnessed the scene and felt the positive energy created by the deep gratitude that they were both feeling.

Our dear disheveled scientist, whose Obsidian had kept evil at bay long enough for our hero to take control of the runaway machine, was blissfully unaware that anything untoward had unfolded there that day at CERN and had carried on tinkering with his machinery long into the evening, very happy with the results that his little weather machine was producing. I could not leave the facility without first planting the seed in his mind, that this machine should be his crowning glory and that he would find love and respect from all quarters in this work, should he harness it purely for the betterment of weather conditions in order to improve life on Earth for the poorest and most deprived and to obliterate its ability to create drought or tumult. He shuddered at the very thought to start with, but it's amazing what grows when you plant the right seeds in furtile soil.

We didn't even bother to follow up on the fate of 'The Atom Smasher', by paying him a visit, since he didn't deserve any such attention from us, nor anyone else should the truth be told. I believe that he lived, but never returned to work, since he had rather let himself down that day, one way or another and he knew it. His illness had also been quite catastrophic and had affected his ability to speak or to walk. He contented himself with reading and commenting on the work of others and even now he could be very tetchy and acerbic with those comments.

Months passed by, after that day, before we caught up properly with everyone again. My twin and I had been on an Atomic vacation, the sort that took us to the far-flung corners of the solar system, showing off our knowledge to each other. It's amazing what fun two almost identical

214

Atoms can have when they are focused on the end result of finding nothing but light relief from the stresses that such an experience brings. We didn't pass through anyone in those months, as we decided that our focus should just be on us and catching up on millennia of missing stories. I was determined to discover whom my twin had foolishly fallen in Love with whilst I had been swooning stupidly over Venus and was not surprised to find that it was Mars. So many of our experiences turned out to be the mirror of, or the shadow to the others light.

We became aware of where our photographer had found herself safe enough to be able to re-emerge, when we saw a poster on The London Underground, for an exhibition of phenomena captured in the lens of our magical snapper titled: 'Run for Your Lives; Seeing the Unseen', to be held at the Science Museum in London and opening in the Spring. She must have fallen on her feet as to whom she had decided to entrust her secrets to, someone of equal status and power to those who would have happily destroyed life on Earth and we applauded her for her agility in navigating such a corrupted and tumultuous modern world, but then we also had to acknowledge that it was ever thus. Man is essentially corruptible and sadly there are always those that cannot be trusted, but there is also good in the world. The people she had found had made sure that all of her images were launched upon the world in a blaze of glory and with the support and fascination of the scientific establishment, who had to acknowledge that their naivety had almost cost us The Earth.

We went to the opening of the exhibition and recognised ourselves in her images alongside many and varied energetic beings made up of energy and light. She did include some of the darker images too, but not the worst of them, since she doubted that anyone would be able to cope with what that meant, or the effects that they might have on the viewer, even in pictures. The most revealing images were gifted to a scientific team headed up by Pale Physics Student, whose job it became to decide how best to proceed at keeping that side of the world in check for as long as possible and so he did do just that, devoting his life to keeping Evil at bay, working closely with Lurking Photographer and eventually on her graduation, his Moody Blonde joined the team too, since they knew better than any on Earth, what they were up against.

The End.

Printed in Great Britain
by Amazon